NOTHING BUT
THE TRUTH

Samuel Lock was born in 1926. He has worked as a painter and stage designer, and as a scriptwriter in the documentary cinema. He is the author of five plays and one previous novel, *As Luck Would Have It*, for which he won the Sagittarius Award in 1996.

Samuel Lock

NOTHING BUT THE TRUTH

V

VINTAGE

Published by Vintage 1999

2 4 6 8 10 9 7 5 3 1

Copyright © Samuel Lock 1998

The right of Samuel Lock to be identified as the author of
this work has been asserted by him in accordance with
the Copyright, Designs and Patents Act, 1988

First published in Great Britain by
Jonathan Cape in 1998

Vintage
Random House, 20 Vauxhall Bridge Road,
London SW1V 2SA

Random House Australia (Pty) Limited
20 Alfred Street, Milsons Point, Sydney
New South Wales 2061, Australia

Random House New Zealand Limited
18 Poland Road, Glenfield,
Auckland 10, New Zealand

Random House South Africa (Pty) Limited
Endulini, 5A Jubilee Road, Parktown 2193,
South Africa

Random House UK Limited Reg. No. 954009

A CIP catalogue record for this book
is available from the British Library

ISBN 0 09 926866 3

Papers used by Random House UK Ltd are natural,
recyclable products made from wood grown in sustain-
able forests. The manufacturing processes conform to the
environmental regulations of the country of origin

Printed and bound in Norway by
AIT Trondheim AS, 1999

for

Adrian de Menasce

and for

James Merrill

I had arrived then at the conclusion that in fashioning a work of art we are by no means free, that we do not choose how we shall make it but that it is pre-existent to us and therefore we are obliged, since it is both necessary and hidden, to do what we should have to do if it were a law of nature, that is to say discover it.

Marcel Proust

PART ONE

I

IN THE LATE evening, after he had eaten at a small restaurant just off the King's Road – in London, that is, in Chelsea – Jason made his way towards the river, and towards a tall dark rambling turn-of-the-century building, in which he had lived for the past three years; renting from the man who lived below – a rather eccentric old gossip who claimed to know everyone in the area – a suite of rooms that overlooked the garden at the back: a garden so unkempt and so uncared-for that, to Jason's mind, whenever he sat before it to write, and at a sturdy, gate-legged table that he would sometimes use as a desk, it offered a space he found quite valuable, and one that he had almost grown to like.

Why should this be – or, rather, why should this have been? Why should this middle-aged man, whose forty-fifth birthday had been a few weeks ago, take pleasure in a garden that could only be called a ruin? Did he perhaps see in its wild disorder some reflection of his inner life?; see in its unchecked weeds that had pushed their way between the cracked stones of its pathways, or in its riot of unpruned briars and brambles that overhung the tops of its crumbling, grey-pink walls, some uncared-for garden within himself that was now claiming his attention; but before which, as if he might be some reluctant, hesitant gardener, who is too daunted by his task, he had been putting off that moment when work on it must begin?

Whatever, he had spent the day alone; not answering his doorbell in the late morning; nor his telephone, which had rung a while after that: and he had passed much of the afternoon amongst the shoppers in the King's Road, glad to be physically close to people he didn't know, and most of whom (there were just a few local faces that were familiar to him) he had not seen before in his life. How deeply sad and strangely sorry he felt as he made his way home through the darkening streets. He was bearded, tall – or tallish, rather – and was now excessively overweight; which partly accounted, he half thought to himself, for why he was feeling so depressed. Food had become for him a consolation of sorts. He didn't smoke, at least; or only occasionally – and only when in the company of other smokers – but he did like to eat and to drink: enjoying going out to restaurants for a good meal (for he seldom ate at home) and clinging to the social contacts he could gain from this: the greetings from the staff who knew him as he came in, and a number of whom had known him for some years (for he had lived a long time in the area); and who often wondered why it should be that, after the brief exchanges as he arrived, and after the generous tips he gave as he left, he never paused to converse: to speak of who he was, or where he lived, or of what his occupation might be. And they had come to accept this; to think of him as 'The Mystery Man' (the nickname they had coined for him). Someone polite; someone authoritative in his way; but surrounded by some curious aura of shade, as though he might be the guardian of some secret.

This view of him was to a certain extent a truthful one. Not that he had any secret to hide – or none that he was conscious of, at least – but he was certainly in hiding from himself; not wanting to know – perhaps not being able to know – exactly who he was; and depending more and more upon the externals of daily life; such as the letters that he would receive from his readers or from his publisher (for Jason was a writer); and upon the steady, careful replies he would send in a small, neat, elegant script; the proportions of which were in such contrast to the general weight and scale of his physique.

In fact, for people who didn't know him at all, receiving one of these carefully written messages of his would give the impression that their sender must be some rather slender, masculine figure who has everything under control: whose cabin is neat, orderly and trim, and in which all is what one calls 'shipshape'.

They – meaning the letters – would give no suggestion to their readers of Jason's physical build; of how he was something of a bull or of an ox; and of how he would almost moan aloud at times in the street; and of how, when it was full, he might sometimes pause to look up at the moon; then, having been drawn by its dreamy light, would submit to drifts into the unconscious that most people would be nervous of and be anxious to avoid.

This ungovernable side of his nature appeared to be now gaining in power. When young, it had been easily pushed aside. He had always been quick of mind; always been able to sum things up; been able to analyse; to assess. And these qualities were reflected in the books he had written; one, a biography of an obscure poet by the name of Andrew Bron; and the rest, stories – novels, that is – all with an excellent sense of surface. Not that easy to read, perhaps, but intelligent, accomplished pieces of writing, in which the characters had a quirky kind of liveliness, even if the books as a whole lacked depth. They were well planned, well thought out: the plots not too complicated – with, occasionally, the suggestion of something larger about to break through: particularly when he was writing of family matters.

But none of his characters ever grew to any real size. Nothing in his books was ever larger than himself. He was never possessed by his subject. It was always kept at a distance. The control – the order – was what he relied upon; what he valued; what he could never give up.

And it had reaped its rewards for him, in that he had quickly found a publisher, which in turn had brought him some fame. Of a limited kind, perhaps, but fame nonetheless. For his books were always well received by the brighter of the critics. 'Another fine piece of writing', would be the type of comment he would receive. 'Intelligent, well planned – a book you should read'; which could almost sound as if the reviewer was saying to his readers that Jason was performing a public service: that he was maintaining a standard of good writing – of decent literature. Indeed, at one moment, he had been quite a fashionable novelist. Not exactly the literary sensation of London, but certainly belonging to what was thought of as the upper bracket of writers.

'Jason Callow's third and most recent novel,' one critic had written a few years ago, 'is that rare thing these days – a work of real intelligence. For those who enjoy books and reading, this novel must be highly recommended.'

So why should he be feeling sorry for himself? Was it because of his life, rather than his work? Because he was now living alone; and because some time ago – it was now a little over three years – his wife had suddenly left him without reason (or at least with none that Jason would admit to or acknowledge) and because his two children, who were now in their teens, only came to visit him occasionally, however much (he would sometimes say to himself untruthfully), he might beg and plead for their company? Or was it more for some other reason; one that Jason couldn't quite touch upon, but that nagged away at his mind; and that drove him towards these irrational moments of depression, when, as has been said, he would moan aloud to himself in the street: as he did now; pausing as he walked along, and with his arms clasped tightly across his chest: and letting out a deep, disturbing noise, that sprang from some inner point of his being.

'Jason, is that you?' a voice called out, as Jason stepped into the hallway of the building where he lived. 'Been out again – have you? Out with your arty-tarty friends?'

Jason didn't reply to this, knowing the voice to be that of his landlord, who had a habit of checking on his movements in this way; and knowing as well that the best way for him to cope with this was to use the defence of silence.

'The doorbell's been ringing,' the sharp voice continued, as Jason began to trudge his way up the stairs. '*Your* doorbell; so I knew you weren't in.'

By this time, Jason had reached the first-floor landing of the house, where, in a flood of yellow light, his landlord stood in the open doorway of his apartment; his gingerish hair – certainly a wig, Jason always thought – almost matching the blotchy colours of his complexion, and the slightly heavier, but still gingerish, tones of his narrow, small, pursed lips.

'I've been out to supper,' Jason said, pausing; and as if to indicate that he wasn't prepared to discuss what he had been doing – or not in detail, at least – and that he would be continuing on his way towards his rooms.

'Putting on weight, you know,' his landlord spat out at him. 'Stuffing yourself. That's what you're doing.'

'Mind your own business,' Jason half muttered in reply – a remark that he always held in reserve until he thought it to be necessary.

'Oh, I'm not prying, dear. Your business is your own. I was just being friendly, Jason – that's all. I wanted to tell you that someone had called. Someone who's not been here before; not as far as I know, that is. Niceish-looking bloke. Quite young too. I went down, you see; and answered the door. Asked if I could take a message. But the sweet, dear thing said no.'

As Arnold said this (Arnold being the name of Jason's landlord), Jason began to wonder who the caller might be. His friends – what friends he had – were more or less of an age similar to his own; and few of them ever came to call at his door. It certainly couldn't be a painter he knew – an artist – by the name of Joseph Mallory, because he would always telephone rather than call; and they usually met out at a local pub. And it certainly couldn't have been his older brother, Jeremy, because he too would never call at the house without having arranged to do so beforehand.

'Didn't know you liked boys, Jason,' Arnold now added with a snigger, '– young men. But there's no knowing people's tastes, dear – is there? Not that it's any concern of mine.'

'Whoever it was, they'll call again,' Jason threw back at him, as if to say that that would be the end of the matter; '– if they want to find me in, that is . . . Goodnight, Arnold. Did you get the post I brought up for you this morning?'

'Yes, dear, I did . . . Thank you. You're so *good*, Jason. A real saint you are. Those stairs are such a bother to me.'

Once Jason had installed himself in his rooms, and had taken off his jacket and had made himself some coffee, he began to reflect upon Arnold's brief description of the man who had called at his door – which, as we know, amounted to nothing more than that he had been young and quite good-looking; and which, as one can imagine, was much too vague and much too general a description to suggest any particular kind of image.

'But the point *is*,' Jason then said to himself, mulling the

8

matter over in his mind, 'that I really don't know *anyone* under forty – not a soul. Except my nephew, perhaps, Alan. It could have been him, I suppose. Perhaps he's in trouble.

'But what *kind* of trouble?' he went on, turning the matter over a second time. 'Got some girl pregnant? Owes money? Quarrelled with his parents? It could be anything – blast it – *any*thing!'; with which he rose swiftly to his feet, slapped his thighs vigorously, and began pacing about his room. His bedroom, that is, where all his books and papers were stored; and that were stacked messily in bookcases and in piles upon the floor.

With it being an evening in early August, it was still not yet quite dark; and for this reason, Jason had switched on none of his lights; and from a window to which he had now crossed, he could see a part of the garden below: a corner of it that was wilder and even more derelict than the rest; and where a large, earthenware bowl lay broken across its pathway; and where, above the broken tops of its walls, the snakelike branches of a briar bush swayed eerily to and fro, in the gentle summer breeze that had now blown up from the river.

That night – some few hours later; and not long after he had gone to bed and had gone to sleep – Jason awoke with a start, feeling disturbed. Had someone entered his room? he wondered. Was someone standing close to his door or by his bed? Or was it more some elusive, ghostly figure that he had encountered in his dream-life; but which, when he awoke, had swiftly vanished?

He could hear voices below, and glancing at an alarm clock that stood facing him, and that perched upon a narrow, painted shelf beyond his bed, knew that Arnold must have company and was staying up late; which was something he was inclined to do; seldom inviting people until ten o'clock or gone, and after he had pottered about all day in a dressing-gown – a rather shabby one – either looking at old newspapers of his – ones that he had simply not thrown away; or toying with his collection of 'pressies', as he always spoke of them; small, Victorian, china figures, that were brought home by people from the seaside; some of sailors, perhaps, with the words 'A Present from Weymouth' or 'From Portsmouth' painted upon them in gold: and other more curious items; such as the one of a miniature china donkey, the tail of which when pulled would release a yellow tape-measure.

All day long Arnold would play with these various knick-knacks of his, or he would browse through his old newspapers – some of which were even a year or more in age: and with the curtains of his room half drawn; and with the windows closed; and with the odd puff or two of dust that he would disturb from time to time, drifting aimlessly about him through the narrow shafts of daylight. But at night, quite late, he would release himself; and sprucing himself up a little, with a quick dab of cologne behind the ears ('Never on the forehead,' he would say to that); and with a light touch of powder upon the cheeks ('Not too much on the nose, dear,' he would say to that); he would cast a lace-edged cloth over a table; bring out a heavy, crude decanter that he would then fill with cheap red wine; something 'extra', perhaps – which was usually port; some cheese; some potted shrimps, perhaps; and so be ready to 'entertain'.

In the darkness of his room, Jason lay listening to the voices; waiting to hear the sound of Arnold's laughter, that he knew must soon rise to a crescendo – a rhythm with which he was familiar; the voices of the guests then quickly following, exchanging their shallow pieces of gossip about the people who lived in the area – some of whom were titled and not actually known by them in person; and not even known by Arnold, who claimed that he knew everyone.

An odd little band. One regular guest being a thinnish, good-looking woman, with snow-white hair and a complexion to match, who always wore bright, near scarlet lipstick and a crumpled, pudding-shaped hat in either damson red or black; and whose voice, which Jason could now hear, was dark in tone; which made it sound at times as if she might be speaking from the grave.

'My little vampire,' Arnold would call her gleefully. 'A real bloodsucker, she is. You should watch out for that one, Jason,' he would say to his tenant at times.

Occasionally, Arnold, this vampire-lady, and another friend of his − or of theirs, rather − a rather nondescript, middle-aged woman, with a fat, smudged face and a straggle of greying, yellowish hair, would be joined by two young men. Jason had seen them several times, climbing the stairs as he went out; and having let themselves in, it would seem, with a key; and wearing suits that were too small for them; their perky faces moving sharply to and fro, as if prepared for any kind of encounter; their neatly knotted ties (for they were always dressed 'formally') giving them a jaunty air of cheerfulness. But whenever they met Jason, they would affect to be demure; lowering their eyes piously as he passed. 'Good evening,' they might half murmur to him quietly; and then, having glanced at Jason briefly, they would quickly look away.

Jason had convinced himself that these were the true bearers of local gossip; that they were the providers of what Arnold appeared to thrive upon. He could never hear the details of their conversation, of course, since it was only the general noise of the various voices that would filter through to his rooms. But he could imagine it; could imagine the quick squeals of laughter that would accompany their juicy pieces of scandal; such as the one which Arnold had once related to Jason, because he thought it might amuse him, concerning a man who lived nearby – a military man – who had always been a bachelor; but who, to the surprise of all who knew him, had decided late in life to marry.

The story went that the real cause of this man's celibacy was that he was obsessed by women's clothes – their underwear in particular – and that in secret, he would often slip on petticoats and the like; which was something he felt ashamed of and refused to share with anyone. But when in his sixties, it seems that he finally met a lady-friend with whom he fell in love; and when she, not he, proposed that they should wed, he surprised her by saying yes.

'And so you see, my dear,' Arnold had then added with a sharp twinkle in his eye, 'when the actual *wedding* night came, and these two old dears, these two old lovey-doveys, were in some posh hotel on the coast; the colonel, or whatever he was, decided that he would reveal his secret to his lady-love. Not by telling her about it, you see; not by having a good talk with her, as he might have done; but simply by stepping out of the bathroom wearing some rather fetching, black, silk lingerie and a few ribbons in his hair.'

'Well,' Arnold had gone on, 'you would have thought – wouldn't you? – that that would have been the end of the affair; of the marriage, I mean. But no! Not a bit of it! Quite the *con*trary! For the bride threw up her hands in glee; pushed her hubby between the sheets; and said, "Darling, don't *worry*. It is all I ever hoped for."'

It was mainly for the exchange of gossipy stories such as this that Arnold's little night-time band would gather: washing them down with a few glasses of wine, or of port; followed by a few munchings of biscuits and cheese: their parties often continuing into the night – sometimes into the early hours. 'Oh, darling, it's such fun; we do enjoy ourselves,' Arnold would say to Jason at times. 'You really must come down and join us.' But which Jason never did.

To those who know Chelsea well – or rather who *knew* it well, for all this took place some time ago – such gatherings as these will come as no surprise; for in the decade that followed the war (the Second World War, that is) there were a lot of people who entertained on very little. And there have always been a lot of eccentric characters in the area – often ones with a theatrical background; as was the case with Arnold, who claimed that he had at one time been a production-manager in the cinema; and who was always quick to inform people that he knew all the stars of the stage and screen. So offbeat characters belonging to some of the stranger seams of life are simply a part of the area's tradition. There was even one well-known 'host', as people spoke of him, who was said to often receive his visitors in a coffin. Not lying down in it, of course, but sitting upright; his arms waving graciously to and fro as his guests began to arrive; as if he might be Cleopatra in her barge, or, more probably, Queen Elizabeth in her carriage.

And then there was another character – a musician who played in clubs and bars in the West End; and who, on a certain Sunday in each month, would give what he called his 'monthly open-house party' for those who cared to call. However, because he lived on the topmost floor of a building in which there was no lift, he was to be seen perpetually hanging out of a window and throwing down his keys.

Jason enjoyed all this. The other side of Chelsea, which was the one of business people and diplomats, and officials of various kinds, all of whom entertained in a more elaborate fashion; their tables set with care; their rooms decked out with expensive leaves and flowers; was something

13

he almost despised. For not having been born into, or brought up in, what one might speak of as a traditional, middle-class home (in that his parents were both such individuals and didn't belong to any one particular group), he was inclined to see that world in terms of caricature; as one of people who seldom expressed towards each other any really genuine feeling or concern; and who seemed to conduct their lives through a series of gestures they all shared; and that had to do with snobberies of various kinds: usually ones connected with class, or simply with money.

Perhaps to some extent we all do that; and Jason certainly cared a lot about money, in that he was always so very careful with it, and tended to classify the people he met in terms of whether they had much of it or not. Nonetheless, it was his interest in the spirit that really dominated his life; and this was reflected in the few friends he had – almost all of whom were intellectuals of a kind: one being the painter that has been mentioned, Joseph Mallory, who, only a month or so ago, had begun a debate with Jason upon the telephone about what he called the 'rise and fall of Jackson Pollock', the American Abstract-Expressionist painter, whose work he had at first admired, but that he now thought rather dull: and he knew a poet too – someone a little younger than himself, who, unfortunately, no longer lived in London; and also a novelist – a woman-friend, with whom he had once had an affair – as well as a few teachers, whose minds were lively, and who, because of their interest in books and paintings, and in spiritual matters in general, came under Arnold's collective heading of 'Jason's arty-tarty friends'.

II

'EDGAR! . . . CAN YOU spare a moment?'

From a sunlit garden, the voice of Lilian Callow span through one of the tall, open French windows of what had been her father's house in Hampshire; a sturdy, fine-looking building that she had inherited only a few years ago, but in which she had lived both with her father until he had died (her mother having died when she was very young) and with Edgar Callow, her husband, for what would soon be forty years.

'Did you call, Lilian?' her husband asked from inside the house, as he appeared to almost stumble from his study into the drawing-room, and as his eyes peered through the thickish lenses of his spectacles to find the distant figure of his wife, who was carrying a bundle of weeds in her right hand and a garden trowel in her left.

'Yes, dear,' Lilian replied. 'I just wanted to say that I've done all the flower-beds. The whole lot of them; so there'll be no need of weeding for a day or two.'

'Lilian, you work too hard. It could have been left for Gordon to do. What do we pay him for? Or until I got round to doing it myself.'

'Oh, I have to be busy, Edgar. You know that. If a thing needs doing I must do it. Besides, I enjoyed it. See how nice it looks.'

Glancing with pride at the work she had just completed,

Lilian quickly disposed of the trowel and the bundle of weeds, then slipped off the sandals she was wearing to step onto the sunwarmed wood of the polished drawing-room floor.

'Shall we have tea?' she asked, now feeling the effects of her efforts.

'Tea? Why? What time is it?'

'It is almost five, dear. We've both been lost in our two worlds.'

'Oh, well; in that case we should,' Edgar replied, screwing up his nose and pushing up his spectacles. 'We *shall*.'

As Edgar was saying this, a telephone rang in the background, and its sound was then soon followed by a light tap on the drawing-room door; which, being only partly ajar, was now pushed open further by Betty, as she was both known and called; and who (as she was always so quick to describe herself), was something a lot less than a housekeeper, but something a little more than a maid.

'The telephone, Mrs Callow,' she said to Lilian, her eyes taking in the state of Edgar Callow's clothing, and checking to see that no buttons were undone. 'It's Mister Jeremy.'

'Jeremy? Really? At this time of day?'

'Yes, Mrs Callow.'

'I wonder why?'

'He didn't say, Mrs Callow.'

'I'll take it, Betty . . . And Betty, dear, as it is almost five, I think that we should have tea.'

'Certainly, Mrs Callow. Will it be in? Or will it be outside in the garden?'

'Oh, out, I think, while the weather's still good. And Betty, dear, you've no need to be quite so formal with us, you know. As I've said to you so often, neither Mr Callow nor myself would object to your calling us by our Christian names; as we call you by yours.'

'Oh, I don't think I could do that, Mrs Callow, much as I always appreciate your suggesting it. It's too modern. And besides, dignity counts a great deal for me, and calling either of you by your Christian name would constitute a loss of it.'

'Betty! What a way of speaking you have. It's all those books you read. You almost talk like one at times.'

'Well, perhaps I do, Mrs Callow, but I can't see the harm there is in that. Books – or the reading of them, rather – is the only education I've had.'

Lilian gave a quick laugh; one light enough not to offend; and Edgar, having looked at Betty with a reflective eye, made his way towards his study, in order to put away his papers and then to freshen himself for tea.

As she reached the telephone, which was kept in the hall of the house, and where it could be cold and draughty in winter, but where it was now quite pleasantly cool, Lilian paused, reminding herself how there could so easily be friction between herself and her eldest son. Quite the opposite of Jason, she thought, her 'second one', as she always named him; the one she admired so much and with whom she had had such a deep, such an intimate relationship; and whose five books – five novels – were on display in a bookcase in the drawing-room, together with his biography of Andrew Bron, a poet few people had heard of, but which Lilian claimed to have read with interest and insisted she had enjoyed.

'Jeremy, dear!' Lilian's voice trembled a little as she spoke into the receiver. 'What a surprise.'

'I know what you're thinking, Mother. What on earth am *I* doing, ringing you at five o'clock on a Sunday afternoon?'

'Well, it *is* rather unusual, dear. I hope it's not to give us bad news or something.'

'No, Mother. I was just wanting to know if Jason is in

London. I've been ringing him all weekend, but can get no reply. I'm going to be in town on business, on Tuesday, and thought that Jason and I might meet.'

'Well, it would be nice for you both, if you could; but I can't help you, I'm afraid, as we've not heard from Jason for quite a while. He was here three weeks ago, as you know, for his birthday; but we've not heard from him since then.'

'You mean, he hasn't rung; hasn't telephoned?'

'No.'

'Or sent a card even?'

'Oh, a card – yes. But he hasn't called; hasn't rung us – no: which is unusual. I've just taken it that he's been busy; writing or something. In fact, we were half thinking of ringing him this evening ourselves.'

'Well, I'll try again,' said Jeremy. 'I just wanted to know that nothing is wrong.'

'Oh, nothing is wrong,' answered Lilian firmly. 'We'd have known if there was. Jason doesn't hide his troubles from us – or not from me, at least. How is Helen, by the way? How are the children?'

'She's fine. Helen is fine. The children too. Alan has a new girlfriend. They've just gone off to France together. And Poppy – well, Poppy is just growing.'

'Oh, what it is to be young,' sighed Lilian, remembering her own first trips to the Continent. 'Enjoy it while you can, Jeremy. Old age does not come alone, you know; as Betty is always reminding us.'

The pleasantries of this family exchange continued for a while longer, before Lilian returned to the garden, and to where her husband, whose knotted hand had been briskly stirring the teapot, was now pouring out the tea. She told him about Jeremy's various questions regarding Jason; said she might try to ring Jason in an hour or two; expressed her certainty that if something was or had been amiss then she – they – would have heard of it; and that she would have known by instinct as well; and, although tired by her work in the garden that day, felt proud of what she had done, and therefore pleased and glad to have done it.

It must have been some two weeks before this sunny, August day, and therefore a week after his birthday, and after he had been to visit his parents, that Jason met his painter-friend, Joseph Mallory, in the bar of a public house: a local one in Chelsea where they would often meet for a drink, and not a stone's throw from Sloane Square.

As usual, Joseph was dressed scruffily; wearing a pair of paint-splashed trousers and a rather heavy seaman's sweater – not at all suitable for the warm weather; and Jason quite neatly, but 'artily', to use one of Arnold's favourite expressions, in a pair of dark-green corduroy slacks and a crumpled, purple-coloured sports shirt, together with a tie that almost matched. And it was on this occasion that they took up the discussion that had been begun by Joseph on the telephone concerning the painter, Jackson Pollock; whose work, as anyone knows, who knows something about modern art, was part of what had been called the American Abstract-Expressionist movement; and an exhibition of whose large, vigorous canvases had been on show at the Whitechapel Art Gallery, and had become the talk of the town.

Both Joseph and Jason had been to see the exhibition, and Joseph was full of it. He knew that Jason was a little blind to the visual arts, and that although painting interested him, and sculpture too, he responded to both more through his intellect than through his body, as it were – meaning in a haptic sense; which, as far as the visual arts are concerned, is the most direct and immediate form of appreciation. But he knew too that Jason was a good listener and liked to be stimulated by his talk; and there was little that he – meaning

19

Joseph – enjoyed more than having Jason as an audience; and as a kind of testing-ground for his ideas.

Joseph always had a tendency to set himself against things that he felt to be 'of the moment', or that he sensed were about to become fashionable, so his theme that evening was that he had 'seen through Pollock', as he put it; something he had already said to Jason on the telephone; and by which he meant that his admiration for this artist, which, only a week or two ago had been so intense – and, indeed, so very positive – had undergone a sudden change.

The argument 'for' Pollock's work, which was the one used at the time (and that might still be used for it today) was that the seemingly random dribbles of paint that cross and re-cross the canvases, together with the odd smear or the occasional brushstroke, were a means used by the artist for trapping the interior world of the unconscious; which everyone seemed to agree upon as having become an important thing to do; since, due to the experiences of the war, perhaps, it seemed to be a world that people felt a strong need to be in touch with just then, by different means and methods: through the use of the Ouija board, for example; or of tarot cards; or (quite a feature of that moment) the consulting of the *I Ching*, the Chinese Book of Changes, which had been published in a translation by Richard Wilhelm and with an Introduction by Jung.

'You can say what you like,' Joseph had argued, 'but as I see it, Pollock's stuff is nothing but wallpaper. Surface-stuff . . . They' (he was here meaning the critics and writers on art) 'are always speaking about it' (meaning, the Abstract-Expressionist movement in general) 'as being a kind of natural progression – or a logical one, rather; that is the word they use – from Monet's "Water Lily" paintings. Get rid of the water lilies, they all argue; get rid of the depiction, the representation, and the next thing's *got* to be abstract art. Well, that's all balls. It's all nonsense. Mondrian – you know

Mondrian's work, don't you, Jason? – the Dutchman – *he's* already followed that line, from representational to abstract art: and where did it get him? No fucking where: up a blind alley . . . I mean, you can't get rid of the figure – can you? Not if you want rich, deep imagery. You've got to have the complexity of the body. And I tell you – in time it'll be back: the figure'll be in vogue again.'

'But what about landscape painting?' Jason then asked pointedly. 'There aren't figures in that, Joe – or only a few at times – and landscape painting can be great, can't it? Be deep?'

'Oh, yes. Of *course* it can,' Joseph answered a little tetchily, not liking to be caught out by Jason, or to be checked in his flow of expression. 'Turner's one of the greatest painters that ever lived. But he's not abstract, Jason; he's figurative too, in the sense that he uses the imagery of the world around him; how he sees it, that is; or *knows* it, might be a better way of putting it. And *that's* why you can't get rid of depiction, Jason – of representation. You've got to have something to be abstract *about*, it seems to me.'

'So don't you think this new stuff will last? This American painting, for example?'

'Oh, it will last – for a while at least. The money's already been poured into it. Like the work of the Pre-Raphaelites: that's lasted: that's lingered on as a kind of curiosity. But it's not really deep, is it? I tell you, Jason, I've seen through this one. It's too possessed by pattern-making. There's no real drawing in it. It does allow for accident – I'll grant it that – which is no bad thing; but it doesn't work *with* it very much; doesn't have a real dialogue with it.'

'But that's the *point* of it!' Jason answered, his voice suddenly loud, and at the same time thumping the table with his fist and rising swiftly to his feet. 'The *point*, Joe', he repeated, and with a sudden flare of anger in his eye, which made Joseph turn quickly to the other customers in the bar, as if to apologise for his friend's behaviour.

'*Listen*, Joe!' Jason went on, almost shouting, 'I've read somewhere — *officially*, I mean: in the *papers*, I mean, that these — these dribbles, or whatever you call them: these — these scrawls of paint on Pollock's canvases, are meant to be a *direct* — an *immediate* representation of the inner state of things; and surely there's got to be something in *that*. There *has* to be!'

'Bollocks, Jason,' said Joseph, lowering his voice a little, and in the hope that Jason might do the same. 'Inner things,' he continued, almost in a whisper, and as if he might be about to impart a secret, 'inner things, Jason — inner states — are deep, not shallow. Leonardo's cartoon — of the Virgin and St Anne, I mean; take that, for example. Those two bloody women: The Virgin and her mother; all fused into one: the rhythms blending; intertwining; like some great story. There's even a touch of Henry Moore in that, I think. And *that's* what *I* call abstract art. Not this paint-pot stuff . . . I tell you, it's a blind alley: more craft than art. If you get too logical in art, Jason — in painting; in the sense of this leading to that, then you're up the creek, it seems to me. Artists need to follow no rules, Jason: to be devious; and I don't think *that* much of Monet's bloody water-lilies, in any case. I'd sooner have a small canvas by Cézanne, than one of those great sprawling canvases by Monet. There's depth there, all right. There's thought *there* — in Cézanne.'

'Thought?' asked Jason, the word striking him.

'Yes, thought. He was thinking — Cézanne was. Non-stop. Always at it; always applying his mind to problems that needed solving. Always stretching himself; always goading himself on to some new solution. I tell you, *he's* the real giant. And thought's gone by the board. *That's* what's wrong. People don't bloody well want to think any longer,

Jason. They want to "express" themselves; or play games with their fucking intellect. Bah! It's all ego-stuff.'

Jason chuckled a little, unaware that a moment of crescendo had just passed, and offered to buy another round of drinks; wanting to hear more of his friend's chatter, and admiring the way in which he would persist with whatever theme he might be exploring: hanging on to it as a dog does to a bone; shaking it; tossing it about; letting go of it; and then quickly grabbing at it again.

'So, then tell me,' Jason asked as he returned, and as he placed their refilled glasses upon the table; and as he gave a quick, almost lordly wave of the hand, which appeared odd, in that its meaning was difficult to interpret, 'how, Joe, are you going to do it?'

'Do what?'

'Well, if, as you say – as people seem to think – the inner world is something that has to be honoured; that has to be looked at. How are you going to do that?'

Joseph didn't reply to this. Not just because it was a question he couldn't yet answer, but also because he was disturbed somewhat by a curious look in Jason's eyes. Sometimes, when they would discuss and argue, in the way they had just been doing that evening, he had already noticed that something in the rhythms of their talk (it seemed to be more that than the actual subject of their debate) would affect Jason in a particular way; one that made Jason want to withdraw; want to break off their conversation. He couldn't say exactly why – what it was that he was experiencing; but it had already occurred on quite a few occasions, and he was now conscious of it disturbing him.

'I want to go to the john,' Joseph said – covering his emotion with a quick laugh, 'have a leak . . . Be back,' he added, patting Jason lightly upon the shoulder, as Jason looked up at him with little real expression upon his face;

staring at him in the way that an animal does at times: vacantly, that is; as if something, or someone, had suddenly called him away, and had forced him to look inwards.

Because the time between the two World Wars had been so short — a period of little more than twenty years — it is at times difficult to realise that a person of Jason's age, who had lived through and experienced the blight and horror of the Second World War, would in fact have been born during the first one, or in the years that immediately preceded it: so that although one could say, perhaps (one is here speaking superficially, as it were) that Jason was a 'modern' person, in that he had grown up and into adulthood during the years of the nineteen-twenties and thirties, when, due to the advent of the aeroplane and the like, people had become so very animated, and so very forward-looking in spirit; and when people at the seaside, for example, had begun to undress in order to bathe, and to don streamlined bathing costumes, in order to display their 'new age' figures; and when (to say a little more about this) short, 'bobbed' haircuts had suddenly come into vogue, for both men and women alike; his birth — that is to say, Jason's birth — had been at a time when women still wore ankle-length skirts and enormous, cumbersome hats; and when people's houses were still lit by gas, rather than electricity; and were heated by open coal-grate fires; and when the majority of the public still travelled about in horse-drawn vehicles. Which means that, in a way, Jason's arrival in this world, and the time of his childhood years that then followed, were linked to the romance and shadow of the Victorian age. For not even the extreme savagery of that first Great War had dispersed those qualities entirely. The shock of it; its horror; the vast roll-call of its dead; had inevitably smudged or shattered many of those nineteenth-century illusions that still lingered on in people's minds, and had broken through the defensive mask of hypocrisy that had been used by the Victorians against what was really happening in their world, and that would lead, alas, to the disasters that then followed. But there still lingered on in life – as, indeed, it still lingers on in life today (although now, to a very much lesser extent, of course) – remnants of Victoriana, as it is called: that is to say, Victorian influences in general; expressed, perhaps, as it appeared to be in Jason's case (although this is pure speculation, of course), through a certain broodiness of temperament: or through a reluctance to be open about personal matters; or through certain forms of odd, irrational projection, that might be used to disguise a person's actions; or through bouts of drunkenness, or of excessive eating – or, for that matter, of drug-taking: all of which show that no age can ever be really 'new', because an old one must be part of it; must be bound up with it.

It is therefore possible that it had been these deep links he had with the Victorian age that were affecting Jason's behaviour, and that were causing his painter-friend, Joseph Mallory, to think that he was behaving not just oddly at times, but in a way that he could only call 'peculiar'; as if, at moments, such as the one that had just occurred, during their discussion in the bar, Jason would seem to remove himself to some other point in time; one that would isolate him from the present and from the people and places around him.

Had Jason been told that this was so – that this was the effect his behaviour was giving – he would have rejected the idea of it immediately. For the view he had of himself was that he was a totally rational creature and always capable of being objective about things. And he would have reminded one too, no doubt, that the world of reason and of the intellect was the world in which he felt himself to be most naturally at home; and that this was reflected in his writings – which was true.

Gradually, however – meaning during the past few months – he had begun to grow conscious of the fact that this view of himself was not a truthful one: that something inside him was now becoming unruly, and was attempting to claim his attention.

Now that is mostly supposition, of course; for one cannot know what goes on inside another person's head. Only Jason could tell us that. One can observe, of course; one can note the behaviour of others – guess at the causes that lie behind it; compare it to that of one's friends, one's relatives – one's children, even; and one can find parallels to it, perhaps, in certain books or in certain plays; so that one can say of a person that they are 'Hamlet-like', or 'Lear-like', if, in the first example, they are excessively introspective – possibly dangerously so – or if, in the second, they feel betrayed or broken or close to the brink of madness. But one cannot really know what is the deep inner truth about anyone; and the suppositions that one has been making, concerning the behaviour of Jason Callow, are all very general ones, and would most probably have been scoffed at by someone who is a professional in that area – by a psychoanalyst, for example. For they would probably have said that it must have been for some much more personal reason, some much more particular one, that Jason was troubled at that time; to do with his relationship with his mother, perhaps, or with his father; or to do with some very early sexual experience he had had – perhaps an incestuous one – the memory of which had been suppressed, and had been driven into the unconscious.

Whether such a person would have declared Jason to be ill or not, is difficult to say. If one is no expert on such matters, it is difficult to judge when, or at what point, what are obviously unusual mental disturbances become a serious form of sickness; one that can be named. One can only relate the things that have been related here so far, and that have provided the subject-matter for the opening pages of this book; which is that this man – this author – who had had some success in life as a writer; who was now in his mid-forties, and whose wife had suddenly left him for no reason (or for none that he could admit to or acknowledge); who lived in London – in Chelsea – and in part of a large, rambling building, quite close to the river Thames; and who, since visiting them on his birthday, had not telephoned his ageing parents – only sent a 'thank-you' card through the post, had, during the past ten days, been answering neither his doorbell nor his telephone, and, on the few occasions when they met, had caused a friend of his who was a painter, and whose name was Joseph Mallory, to believe that Jason was 'going real bonkers', as he had put it to a friend – the woman-novelist, with whom Jason had once had an affair; who in turn, had spoken of it to other people they knew, two of whom were teachers. But none of these various friends had taken the matter seriously at all; mainly because their experience of Joseph was that his head was always full of such 'scatterbrained' ideas, and that this was probably just another in the lengthy list of his fanciful inventions.

III

'YOU KNOW WHO I mean, don't you, Lottie? You know who I am talking about?'

'Of course I do. I've seen him several times. He's your neighbour; who lives upstairs. He's a writer.'

'Yes, he is. And a very good one, I'm told; but too highbrow for me, I'm afraid, which is why I've never read him. But you know, darling, I don't read very much these days, in any case.'

Lottie, who was Arnold's vampire-lady friend, and who on this weekday afternoon was alone with him for a change; and who, as she spoke, was touching up her lipstick; using a small mirror to do so that she had taken from her handbag – a voluminous one, that had been made from imitation leather – kept moving her head up and down and to and fro; in order to obtain a better view of herself.

'Because of your eyes, you mean?' Lottie asked, as she concentrated intently upon what she was doing.

'Well, yes,' said Arnold. 'I'm not as young as I used to be, you know. And it's not just my eyes that are bothering me, darling, it's my legs as well – they're in a *shocking* state. "Varsicose veins", as my dear old mother used to say.'

'You can have those out,' stated Lottie without expression, and still concentrating upon the view of herself in the mirror.

'Oh, I know *that*, dear. I've been into that. But who'd want to have half their leg cut away? Besides, I don't like doctors. I don't trust them.'

'Anyway, what were you going to say about your neighbour, Arnold?'

'About Jason, you mean? – that's his Christian name, Lottie; his first one – well dear, I was going to say that I think he's rather a dish.'

Lottie paused to stare at Arnold for a few seconds, but didn't respond at all to the wicked twinkle in his eyes.

'Mind you, there's something odd about him,' Arnold went on, 'but – well – I don't think I'd object very much to a night or two with *him*.'

'Not my type,' said Lottie flatly, as she pursed and sucked her lips, to make sure of her lipstick being spread evenly. 'Too hirsute,' she added dryly.

'Because of the beard, you mean?'

'Yes. Not that I dislike *all* beards, Arnold. In fact, I once went out with a naval officer from Portsmouth, who looked like the sailor on the advertisement. For cigarettes, I mean. But for some reason it didn't bother me . . . Perhaps,' she added, lowering her husky voice to an even deeper register than usual, and affecting to speak in a seductive manner, 'because he was "all that a woman could desire".'

'What *you* desire, Lottie, I never know. You pick 'em off like flies, it seems to me – your men. We're opposites there: aren't we, darling?'

Lottie ignored this last remark and snapped her handbag shut; then looked down to see that the seams of her stockings were straight. 'In what *way* is he odd?' she then asked.

'Jason?'

'Yes.'

'Oh, I don't know, dear. He's strange. Some days he

just walks the streets – or so people tell me. Billy and John, for example; they saw him yesterday. He's got friends – a few; but he doesn't see them much; except for a scruffy painter he knows . . . I've got an idea that he's a bit – well, I suppose he's a bit mixed up about something. Mind you, a lot of people seem to be that, these days, what with the war and things. Perhaps I'll have to sort him out. Perhaps I'll have to take him under my wing.'

'Is this on *straight*?' Lottie then asked, catching hold of the brim of her velvet, pudding-shaped hat, and pulling it down at either side, so that it curved a little above the curls of her white-haired fringe. 'Arnold! Is it *straight*? My hat?'

'Yes, it is, dear. You look lovely. You always do. Why *you* don't have a man, I have no idea.'

'He drinks – doesn't he?' said Lottie, again ignoring Arnold's comment, and returning to the subject of Jason.

'Yes, he does. Quite a lot.'

'You can see it. You always can. Violent, probably . . . I wouldn't trust him with a bargepole . . . I mean, he was married, wasn't he? Doesn't he have children?'

'Oh, yes – two: and very nice they are as well. He doesn't see much of them though. But they have been here; once or twice. Teenagers, they are. A boy and a girl.'

'Well,' said Lottie, suddenly straightening herself, and drawing on a pair of long, black cotton gloves, which showed that she was preparing to depart, 'I must be off . . . See you tomorrow, Arnold,' she then added, as she crossed towards the door.

'Tomorrow, yes,' said Arnold, looking at her admiringly, and wishing that he could ape the strong confidence she displayed, 'at ten. And *not* before, Lottie. John and Billy can't be here until late. They're going to the theatre; to a revue at the Royal Court. And Sophie's going to be late as well.'

'Bye, darling,' said Lottie, giving Arnold a careful peck on the cheek, accompanied by a hard, lustrous smile; the violet pupils of her eyes suddenly flashing with silver light; and her eyelids suddenly softening with the moisture of a few tears.

'Bye,' said Arnold, who always welcomed signs of affection; and who, as he closed the door of his room, and as he reminded himself that he should be grateful to have such a friend, determined that the next time he saw Lottie – which, as we know, was to be as soon as the following night – he would give her one of his 'pressies'. 'Perhaps the one from Portsmouth,' he thought to himself with a smile. 'She'll love it. It's got a man on it; a sailor; and it's a bearded one; and his head is outlined in gold.'

'Finished? . . . Yes,' said Betty with a grunt, and as she stooped to remove a coffee cup and saucer from a low, occasional table, close to where Edgar Callow was sitting.

'There'll be little response from *that* quarter tonight, Betty, I fear,' said Lilian Callow, with a nod towards her husband, who, since finishing his after-dinner coffee had been engrossed in reading a book.

'Oh, I can understand *that*, Mrs Callow,' replied Betty. 'Books can be another world, can't they? And you can never tell how lost in them you might become; which is why I like them, I suppose.

'Not all books have that power, Betty; that ability; to make one become lost in them.'

'No, perhaps not. But the ones *I* enjoy seem to have it, Mrs Callow. Perhaps it's because they are all classics. A book can't be a classic, I expect, unless it takes you on some kind of adventure. One of the mind, I mean.'

Lilian smiled, and watched Betty as she deftly stacked the tray she was carrying with the coffee-things; enjoying, as she always did so much, the physical weight of Betty's presence; and of how she seemed never to lose her centre or to become ruffled; although she could become excited at times, when she would go into a 'hot flush', as she always spoke of it, and her cheeks and neck would redden; and when, in order to relieve herself of her embarrassment, she would let out a quick, hearty burst of laughter.

'You certainly do like books,' said Lilian, her eyes following Betty's movements. 'Which is your favourite author, I wonder?'

'My favourite?' replied Betty, pausing for a moment, and looking towards the tall, open French windows, that were allowing a pleasant flow of air to freshen the room. 'Well, I *used* to like Charles Dickens, Mrs Callow. He used to be my favourite. I liked the funny bits, and the eccentricity of some of his characters. But now I seem to have been bitten by George Eliot. A wonderful woman she was, it seems to me. Very serious: isn't she? The book I like best is about a young man who's got no parents. Or at least he doesn't seem to have any at the beginning of the book. Then he meets his mother, and discovers that he's a Jew. It's a wonderful story; but for some reason I can never remember the name of it. It's Daniel something, I think.'

'Deronda,' said Lilian, who had never read the book, but who knew the title of it well.

'Oh, yes. That's right – "Daniel Deronda". It's the sort of story I enjoy. It's all about love and religion, in a way; and some of the scenes have a kind of glow to them, if you know what I mean. They're almost mystical.'

'I'm afraid I haven't read it, Betty,' said Lilian, feeling a trifle ashamed of herself, and in view of Betty's lack of education.

'Well,' said Betty, ignoring Lilian's admission, 'I'd better get these things down to the kitchen, I think. Then it'll be an early bed for once . . . And with one of my favourite books, I expect,' she added with a laugh. 'Oh, words! What would I do without them?'

Lilian wondered what the answer to that might be, as Betty gave her a smile and began to cross the room.

'Oh. And what about Jason?' Betty then asked. 'What happened, Mrs Callow? Did Mr Jeremy manage to speak to him, or what? It's funny your not having heard from him at all. Did you ring him up yourself this evening, as you said you were going to do?'

'No, I didn't,' replied Lilian, who was always glad of Betty's concern regarding such matters. 'Jeremy said he'd ring back, if he got hold of Jason at all and – well – he hasn't. I expect Jason's busy. Writing; or out with some of his friends.'

'Poor Jason,' said Betty.

'Why do you call him that, Betty?'

'Why, Mrs Callow? Because I feel sorry for him – that's why. He's not been right, you know; ever since Jill went off with the children. I think it upset him far more than any of us realise.'

A silence fell between the two women: then they looked directly towards each other, allowing their eyes to meet; and in a way that they seldom did, since it was a deeply intimate look and one that was held in reserve by them both.

'It's hot – isn't it?' said Lilian, taking out a handkerchief from beneath one of the short, cuffed sleeves of the dress she was wearing, and using it to pat her cheeks and her forehead.

'It's August,' answered Betty. 'There's thunder about. There was this morning.'

The silence between them then returned, and Lilian rose to her feet. Then she moved across the room to the windows, and to the view beyond them of the garden that she had tidied and weeded earlier; and where the last, faint glimmer of daylight tipped its trees and bushes with gold.

'Jason is in trouble,' stated Lilian, without turning. 'Something is wrong, Betty. Something is – I don't know – not right.'

'Yes, Mrs Callow. I believe so,' said Betty with quiet, sober authority, as she was about to leave the room; and as Lilian, who had not looked at her again, turned away from the windows and recrossed towards her chair.

'Lilian. Did you speak?' asked Edgar Callow. 'Did you say something?'

'No, dear. Betty and I were just gossiping.'

'Oh,' answered Edgar, going back at once to his book, unconscious of the brief moment of anxiety that had just been shared by the two women; and believing, as he always preferred to do, that the life around him was untroubled.

'I think I'll go to bed,' said Lilian. 'You *will* close the windows, won't you, Edgar?'

Edgar looked up at his wife, his screwed-up features betraying that he had not taken in what she had just said.

'The windows, Edgar,' Lilian repeated. 'You *will* close them.'

'Oh, yes. Yes, of course. Don't worry, Lilian. I'll close them. I'll see to them.'

Lilian crossed swiftly to her husband and stooped to kiss him upon the forehead, then quickly said her goodnights to him and took herself off to bed.

In London that same night, and in the bedroom of their top-floor flat in South Kensington that had been converted from rooms once used by servants, and that was tucked beneath the heavy, mansard roof of what had been a wealthy, Victorian mansion, Arnold's friends, John and Billy, were finding it difficult to sleep.

'Billy, move *over*,' said John, giving his friend a playful push.' 'You take up too much room.'

'I do *not*,' said Billy, who was lying with his hands clasped behind his head.

'Yes, you do,' said John, slipping a hand between Billy's legs, and gently stroking his groin.

'Stop *doing* that!' protested Billy.

'Stop doing what?'

'*That*. You'll get me going, you will.'

'And what's wrong with getting you going?'

'Nothing. It's just not what I want, that's all. Not at the moment, at least. I just want to lie. I just want to think.'

'*Think!* Some hope of that, you old queen.'

'John! Just stop that talk; always making me out to be an imbecile or something. I was thinking about that man – the one at Arnold's; who lives above him. You know who I mean. We've seen him several times – on the stairs.'

'And in the street as well,' added John.

'Yes. We did yesterday.'

'So what about him?'

'What about him? Well. I don't know. I was just thinking about him; wondering if he's queer or something.'

'Queer? Him? That bearded one?'

'Yes. Don't you think he could be? I mean, the way he looks at us. He's never exactly hostile, is he?'

'Look, Billy. All people – all men – who aren't queer, aren't necessarily hostile. You need to know that. My brother isn't, for one. Like me, he thinks the world of you. He thinks you're wonderful.'

'Oh, don't start giving me *that* sort of talk. I know what *that's* for . . . No, seriously, John. I mean it. If he's not queer, in the sense of – well, "queer" – then there's something about him that is definitely what I would call peculiar.'

'Anyway, he's married; or so Arnold says.'

35

'I know, but he's separated – or divorced, perhaps.'

'*And* he's got children.'

'Yes, but so had Oscar Wilde.'

'All *right* – so he left his wife, or she left him, because he's got peculiar tastes in sex – in bed. So what, Billy, is interesting about that?'

'I don't know. It just *is*. People interest me. *All* people.'

'You mean, you've got a crush on him – is that what it is?'

'John, don't be bloody stupid. Don't be –'

John had now slipped his hand up to Billy's stomach, and was gently stroking it – occasionally flicking a finger into his navel, which he knew that Billy enjoyed.

'Tell me now. Do you fancy him?' asked John, teasingly, slipping his free arm beneath Billy's shoulders, and pulling himself close to Billy's body, which, though small, was much more muscular than it gave the impression of being when he was dressed in one of his suits.

'No. I do not.'

'You do, you know,' John teased. 'You fancy him.'

'I do *not*,' insisted Billy, as John now played with Billy's genitals, then took hold of Billy's hand and drew it towards his own penis, which was erect, and of which he was justly proud.

'You don't?' said John. 'So who *do* you fancy, then? Me, for instance? *This*, for instance?'

'Oh, stop being so bloody crude: so bloody filthy.'

'Crude? What's crude about it?'

'Get stuffed,' answered Billy with a laugh.

'That's what *you're* going to be, if you aren't careful,' said John, pressing himself close to one of Billy's thighs.

'Dirty old man,' said Billy, drawing up his knees, and pressing them against his lover's stomach.

'Dirty *young* man, you mean.'

'Dirty *old* young man,' said Billy, slipping an arm around

John's waist, and then stroking the base of his spine. 'You like that – don't you?' he teased in return. 'Don't you, John?'

'Little monkey, you.'

'Big *gorilla*, you,' said Billy.

'Big one?'

'Yes. *Big* one!'

'Better than man with beard on staircase?'

'I expect so,' answered Billy.

'What do you mean – *expect* so? Say you know so.'

'I know so,' said Billy, submissively.

'Say it again. Say "I know so" again,' demanded John.

Billy repeated the phrase and then gave his lover a kiss; which they both took as a sign that the talking between them should cease, and that their love-making should now deepen; the animal side of their natures suddenly asserting itself, and making them seem much simpler and more noble than the nervous, cautious character of their timid, daytime selves; as if they needed and used a mask of defence against the world; one that showed them as being not ugly exactly, but certainly plain and shy and careful; and much less strong and sure, and much less beautiful than they really were; and which was a side of their personalities they never revealed in public: only secretly, to each other: and only at night and when in bed.

And perhaps there are a great number of couples of whom this could be said to be true. Perhaps people are more shy of their deeper, animal natures than they are aware – or more shy of disclosing them in public, at least. And perhaps masks of a kind, such as the ones that were adopted by John and Billy, are a necessary feature of modern life, when, due to the intensity of its pressures it would seem that anyone, at almost any time, can so easily become the object of another person's projections.

Whatever, these two young lovers now enjoyed themselves; and with the weather being so hot, were glad to be rid of sheets and blankets for a change; and to be able to make love beneath the stars, as it were, with their bedroom window wide open; and with the huge thunderclouds of August passing slowly towards the West; and with the early throb of traffic, that had now begun in the Cromwell Road, where people were already on the move; either driving into the city from the suburbs, or out towards the airport and beyond.

A while later, at Arnold's house in Chelsea, after John and Billy's love-making had ceased, and after they had at last fallen asleep, Jason again awoke with a start, believing, as he had done the previous night, that someone had stepped into his room and was standing close to his bed.

This time, however, no voices could be heard, since Arnold was alone, not having arranged to have another of his little 'gatherings' until the evening of the next day: which was to be late – 'gone ten' – as we know, and after Billy and John had been to the theatre, to a revue at the Royal Court; which is the very last place where one would expect to see such a type of entertainment today; but where, in the nineteen-fifties, there were occasionally smart, witty revues of an extremely sophisticated kind, in which songs were sung and jokes were made about all sorts of fashionable people; including, as one recalls, jokes about Benjamin Britten.

Nonetheless, if no voices could be heard, there was an unfamiliar light flooding up from the garden below, which Jason thought must be coming from the windows of Arnold's apartment – who, he imagined, might not have bothered to draw his curtains and had fallen asleep in a chair; both of which were things that he had done occasionally in the past, and which caused Jason concern, thinking, as he always did, that Arnold could easily be unwell – or, indeed, could possibly be dead.

This latter thought was an over-dramatic one, of course, and Jason was aware of it. But he knew that Arnold was older in years than he said, and certainly older than he looked; and he knew as well that even if he had been taken ill, he would have been too proud to call for help. 'If I have to go,' he had been known to remark, 'they'll find me in the morning.'

In those days – in the nineteen-fifties – it was the habit of the majority of men to wear pyjamas when in bed; either thin cotton ones in the summer, or thicker, perhaps partly woollen ones, during the colder months of the year. But in this respect, Jason was quite modern in his ideas, in that he usually slept in the nude; or if not in the nude, then at least in only his underpants. And in the event of his feeling cold at all during the night – when he went to the lavatory, for example – he kept a dressing-gown close by him that he usually had draped across his bed.

Now, with it being August, and with the weather being so hot, he was glad that he was naked; and he felt no need to reach for his dressing-gown as he hauled himself out of bed: thinking only that he really *must* do something about Arnold: that he must either go down and call at his flat, or he must try to speak to him on the telephone.

Because of the glow of reflected light that was spilling gently into his room, Jason had switched on no light of his own; and as he went to collect his shirt and his trousers from where he had left them the night before, he caught sight of himself in a mirror.

As was said at the beginning of this book, Jason was reasonably tall, and had he been fit, and had his body been trim, one would have said too that he was a decent-looking, quite imposing figure of a man. Instead, however, he could now see in the glass that whilst his shoulders weren't at all hunched, and were still quite decently shaped, there was a truly ugly tyre of fat around his middle; and his thighs, which he thought of as being still muscular and firm, were also showing signs of excessive flesh; so that above his knees, which in themselves appeared to be swollen, there were hints of loose, ungainly folds that drooped towards his kneecaps.

Perhaps because no light had been switched on, and because he was exposed to only a half-light as a result, Jason drew closer to the mirror in order to obtain a better view of himself; and as he did so, his legs and torso moved swiftly out of focus, and it was only the uppermost part of his body that he now found himself confronting.

Could it be, he half wondered, that there was a curious twist in his face?; as if one half of it had been lifted up, and been placed at a higher level than the other? His beard at least was trim – or was reasonably so. For some reason, he was able to attend to that. But his dark, auburnish hair was even more unruly than usual, and to the left of his head, and therefore to the right of it in the mirror, a quick, savage thrust of mane made him appear to be unbalanced. Even more curious were his eyes. In spite of his skin being sallow, it was a little pinkish at the same time, and he now noticed what appeared as a thin blue or greyish line, that seemed to follow the edges of his eyelids and then push towards his nose; and from there to curl beneath his nostrils. And the eyes themselves looked tired. Circling the deep marbled green of their pupils, the whites were marked with a network of scarlet veins; and there also appeared to be yellow, or lemonish patches on his cheeks, and a few similar such patches on his forehead.

'Probably the drink,' Jason muttered to himself, knowing that he would do nothing about it, and that the nightly bottle of wine, combined with the glass or two of spirits that he drank earlier each day, had become a necessary feature of his life – a built-in feature of it, that is; as the eating had done, and as had the lack of any vigorous form of exercise.

It was therefore not with a shrug of indifference exactly, but one that simply said 'so be it', that Jason finally left the mirror, and the new picture that had been given to him, and swiftly began to dress; pulling on a shirt and slacks, and slipping into a pair of lightweight summer shoes; then collecting his keys from a bedside table before quickly leaving his rooms in order to descend to the first-floor landing; intent upon discovering why it should be that the light from Arnold's windows was spilling into the garden; and hoping against hope, as they say, (for Jason disliked all moments of high drama) that it would be for no different reason than that Arnold had fallen asleep in a chair; having left his lights switched on; and having forgotten to draw his curtains.

IV

WHETHER OR NOT an author should be expressing philosophical thoughts and ideas in a novel, is perhaps open to
question, since the purpose of it – of novel-writing – is
the telling of a tale, or of a story – the constructing of a
narrative, that is – that will draw the reader into another
world; one in which he or she can become lost for a
few hours, and so removed for a while from the world
of daily life. Or that will surely be most people's idea of
such a book; and will be the reason, no doubt – or will
be the main reason – for their purchasing works of fiction.
Indeed, quite recently, some writer said on the radio (this
was quite a well-known writer, one might add) that not
only did they not care for, but they actively rejected and
despised, what they spoke of as 'think bits' in a novel (by
which one presumed they meant reflective comments and
asides); but which does away, alas, with vast stretches of
modern fiction; with a great deal of Proust's writing, for
example, and with the work of a great many other writers
besides.

Yet surely there has to be room for such things in a novel.
If not for ones that are of a philosophical nature exactly,
then surely there has to be room for psychological ones, at
least; since the novel has so much to do with the character
of people – or, to be more precise, with the character
of characters (for they are never 'real' people, are they?);

and also because the psychic or subjective world that lies beneath the mask of daily life, and in which all action appears to be rooted, and from which it all inevitably springs, is now such a part of modern-day consciousness that it would be quite the opposite of modern if one were to exclude such comments entirely.

And in any case, they – meaning such comments and asides – can add perspective to a tale; can supply the narrative with subsidiary routes and byways that can help the reader to gain a better view of it. For example, a word-picture has been painted here of Jason Callow that shows him as being a man under considerable strain, and who appears to be cut off from, and so out of touch with, some aspect of his being that had begun to become unruly, as if it might be protesting at its neglect. But on the other hand, one hasn't yet ventured to say (although it would certainly add perspective to the story if one did) what exactly that protesting part of Jason's nature might be.

This, unfortunately, is partly because (as has already been said) it is only Jason himself who could have told us what went on inside his head – or went on inside his mind, rather. All that one has been able to do is to show just a few of what one might speak of as the outer symptoms of his distress, and how the ripples caused by that disorder (and which, as we have seen, had begun to disturb him) were also beginning to affect and disturb the people around him in his life: Joseph, his painter-friend, for example, who thought that Jason was going 'real bonkers': his landlord, Arnold, who was concerned about his walking the streets such a lot and spending so much of his time alone: Billy, who was definitely of the opinion that Jason was what he would call 'peculiar'; and also, of course, his parents, who hadn't heard from him – or hadn't heard his voice, at least – for weeks; ever since he had been to visit them on his birthday.

It is true that at one point – and this was another example of creating perspective – one did risk saying that because of his age (meaning, because of the time at which he had been born), Jason's moodiness, combined with his compulsive intake of food and of drink, could possibly have their roots in certain of the messy leftovers of the Victorian age – the psychological ones, that is: but this was said just to offset any assumptions that may have been made that Jason's problems were only personal ones; as opposed to ones rooted in a collective source. And one did that – said that – because there is such a lot of that type of thinking today, that believes that the roots of all mental disorder can be traced back either to the years of our early childhood, or to things that happened to us in puberty. And whilst it is obvious that there are certain truths that may be arrived at through that type of reductive thought (in that we are all inevitably partly formed and partly moulded by things that happen to us when we are young), it seems to be equally obvious that there is something else, something that has nothing to do with worldly experience whatsoever, that is at play upon our lives: something of which we are at first completely unaware; but which, as time goes by, plays itself out *through* us, so to speak. As if every person – as if each individual had his or her story to tell; or not 'tell' exactly, since that sounds as if we are inventing the story ourselves; but that wants to tell itself *through* us, whether we like the idea of it or not.

And most of us (this is just a personal view, of course) will attempt at times to reject some part of our story, whilst at others, we grasp hold of our story gladly. But the really big, the really dramatic moments of psychic turbulence in our lives, are provoked, it would seem, when (perhaps through a stubborn imposition of the will) a person actively chooses to *suppress* a part of their true story; and through doing that, to suppress a part of their true self. Which, it would appear, looking at it only from the outside, is what had happened to Jason Callow: he had failed – indeed, had perhaps even refused – to grasp hold of his full story, and had severed himself, as a result of that, from what one might call the 'narrative' of his true self – which, considering that he was a writer – *and*, moreover, a novelist – had put him in a dangerous position; for it meant that his books – his novels – were in fact literary lies: untruthful cover-ups of a kind; that were being bought by members of the public who gladly subscribed to what he had done, and who were giving it their support.

Jason had already knocked a number of times on the door of Arnold's apartment; and having received no reply, was wondering whether he should return to his rooms and try the telephone, or perhaps knock yet again even louder. Then he suddenly recalled how he had once seen Arnold stoop to slip a key beneath a narrow run of stair-carpet that passed in front of his door; and to Jason's surprise (for he hadn't a clear memory of the exact position) he found the key almost immediately and was able to enter the flat.

As Jason opened the door to let himself in, the soft light of Arnold's rooms (that flowed from a series of lamps whose shades were all faded and torn, and that were amber with age and with use) flooded past him onto the landing. And as he then turned to close the door, he saw how his shadow caught at the far wall of the stairwell, then raced to gigantic proportions; as it grew quickly; and where he watched it nervously for a while, before turning to the light and warmth of the interior, which smelled oddly sweet, he noticed; perhaps even a trifle sickly; and might have been due, he thought, to the lingering smell of a popular, cheap cologne that Arnold used: or of incense, perhaps, that he would burn from time to time.

As Jason passed from the small entrance-hall into the

main living-room of the flat, where Arnold's collection of knick-knacks were displayed – all in glass-fronted cupboards that weren't of very good quality, and some of which had bow-shaped doors, and intricately fashioned handles, that were made of brass perhaps, but that had now become blackened with neglect – he noted, for the first time, that above and at either side of these cupboards, and all hanging by faded, velvet ribbons from a sturdy wooden picture-rail, were a number of large, metal-framed photographs of early stars of the British cinema – Margaret Lockwood and the like. 'To Arnold with all my love', being the type of message written across them; or 'To Dearest Arnie – love you ever' – followed by a signature not quite readable; but judging by the size of the scrawly handwriting, one of someone now quite old; whose features, if one could now see them, would bear no resemblance whatsoever to those of the smart, matinée-idol figure that peered at one out of the picture-frame.

Arnold hadn't fallen asleep in a chair, he had fallen from one; and lay stretched out upon the floor with his arms flung to either side; his chin sticking upwards into the air; and with his hairpiece half free of his head – which meant that the gingerish tones of his complexion changed suddenly as they passed upward from his forehead to the almost lurid pink of his scalp.

Jason knew at once that Arnold was not dead. How he knew it he couldn't be sure: perhaps the memory of dead bodies that he had experienced in the war, when in the army: perhaps too because the room felt strangely alive; and also because he could smell that the heat of Arnold's body was releasing the odour of the cheap perfume that he was inclined to use so lavishly: and perhaps as well, because Jason had noted in his mind that there were heavy beads of perspiration on his forehead.

46

Had Arnold been drinking? Jason wondered. He certainly liked the odd nip or two of whisky, or the occasional glass of port or of wine: but he wasn't a real drinker. His breathing, however, was steady, and Jason felt quite confident that he had suffered no stroke or sudden collapse of that kind; and half imagined that he had probably been singing old love-songs to himself – or crooning them, would be a better way of describing it. For he was always reminiscing about what he called the 'good old days' before the war, and singing songs from Astaire-Rogers films, or ones made famous by Bing Crosby. 'Let's Face the Music and Dance' being a favourite of his; or 'Deep Purple' (how he loved the line, 'over misty garden walls'); and he would often sing with a kind of chuckle in his throat, a song that he learned later, called 'Kiss the Boys Goodbye', into which he threw great meaning and innuendo.

As Jason's mind went swiftly through these various thoughts, Arnold suddenly opened his eyes and looked directly up at him.

'Jason! How *nice* to see you,' Arnold said to him with a smile. 'Won't you –'

'Arnold, you've fallen; from your chair or something. Are you all right?'

'All *right*, dear? I'm in seventh heaven.'

'Yes. But I mean – have you hurt yourself?'

'Hurt myself?' said Arnold, now quickly fumbling with his hairpiece and pushing it back into position. 'Just letting me hair down, dear – that's all that it was. Drunk a little too much for once, I'm afraid. You shouldn't have bothered to come down, you know. Very kind of you and all that; but I'd have got myself off to bed eventually.'

'The lights were on,' said Jason.

'The lights?'

'Yes. You'd forgotten to draw your curtains, and the

47

light from your windows was spilling into the garden and from the garden into my rooms.'

'Oh, well. I don't always draw them in the summer, you know, when it's so hot . . . Still, it was very nice of you to bother, Jason: to be concerned. A real saint you are.'

Jason didn't reply to this. He *was* concerned; but didn't quite want Arnold to think that he was; so he gruffly told Arnold to catch hold of him firmly by the arm, and pull himself to his feet; which he did, obediently, and with comparative ease. And then, without either of them speaking to the other, Jason guided Arnold into his bedroom; asked if he could get himself to bed: was assured quite assertively that he could, if Jason would just switch the lights off in the living room and the hall: and then, without any further exchange between them, Jason left.

PART TWO

V

'JEREMY! WHERE IS Jason?'

'I don't know, Betty.'

'But I thought you went out to play together.'

'We did; but I wanted to see to my bicycle; and Jason ran off – down to the river.'

'Well, go and fetch him – there's a good boy.'

'Do I have to?' asked Jeremy, who was about to fix a patch on the tube of his bicycle tyre.

'You don't *have* to,' answered Betty, diplomatically, 'but lunch will be on the table soon; and you know how anxious your father will be if you're late.'

'I'm *never* late,' said Jeremy, defiantly.

'I know – I meant Jason. So please go down and fetch him. He'll be in a mess, I expect. He's such a mucky boy.'

Jeremy responded with a smile, then bounded off, watched lovingly by Betty, whose favourite he was, and who had been recently noticing with pride how sturdy he had become; and at the back of whose mind a consciousness had been forming that he was about to become a man; and of the changes this would bring to her life; in that their relationship would change, and that it was something for which she should be preparing herself.

Beyond the gardens of the house, that were kept so orderly

and trim, a narrow path led through the tangled branches of a small orchard to the sudden sweep of an open meadow; and then beyond that, to the curving banks of a broad river, where the two boys had played together so often when they were small; and where now, as he approached, Jeremy could see Jason standing upon a large stone, with the water swirling about it; and concentrating, it would seem, upon some particular action, for his eyes stared fixedly downward.

Before calling out to say that lunch was about to be ready, Jeremy paused – slowing down in pace and walking with caution; half hoping that his brother hadn't heard his approach. Then, as he drew close to the river bank, he saw that Jason had caught a fish – quite a large one – and had placed it beneath one of his shoes, pressing it firmly against the stone upon which he was standing.

'Now then,' Jeremy heard his brother say, '*you* are going to die. *I* am going to punish you. *I* am going to kill you.'

Disturbed by the intensity of Jason's voice, Jeremy stopped and kept still.

'Kill you! – that's what I'm going to do,' Jason suddenly blurted out, '– 'till the blood runs out: 'till I see the *blood*, do you hear?' – with which he stooped to plunge a hand into the water and to select a small, well-rounded stone from the river-bed. Then, using it, he began to batter the struggling creature to death.

In the sharp, midday sunlight, the silver of fins and scales sent out quick flashes of light, as the fish squirmed and struggled in the grip of Jason's shoe. Then the blood began to flow; the silver to become stained with scarlet: the scarlet escaping into the water; then dissolving, as the current bore it away.

'Jason!' Jeremy shouted angrily. 'What are you *doing*? Why are you doing that?'

Jason looked up at him with no sign of understanding

in his eyes. Then, as he seemed to return from some cut-off area of the mind, he smiled: not in a silly or stupid manner exactly; but it was a distant and impersonal smile; and one that appeared to express some unusual form of satisfaction.

'It's dead,' he said, looking down at the now lifeless fish. 'I killed it.'

'I must say, Betty,' remarked Lilian Callow, 'I am always glad when lunch is over. For some reason, I get more done in the afternoons.'

'Well, there we're opposites, Mrs C. All I can think of after lunch is having a snooze. I'm more of a morning person, I suppose.'

'Yes, you are, Betty. You always have been.'

Betty laughed when Lilian said this, and began to tidy the corner of the dining-room, where she had been putting away some cutlery that she had just brought in from the kitchen.

'Betty,' said Lilian, 'you looked flustered at lunch. Were the boys late or something?'

'Not Jeremy,' said Betty, 'but Jason almost was. He'd been down to the river and had caught himself a fish. Such a mess he was in too. There were spots of blood all over his trousers.'

'Blood?'

'Yes. From the fish. Jeremy said he'd trampled upon it; then battered it with a stone. Kept saying he'd killed it.'

'Oh, my! That sounds rather savage – doesn't it, Betty? How did he manage to catch the fish, I wonder?'

'With his hands, Mrs Callow. Tickles them, he does – then grabs at them. He says he's seen the poachers do it.'

'Well, I don't think we should be encouraging him in that sort of thing. You know how Mr Callow and I dislike blood sports – of any kind: if fishing can be said to be one.'

'Oh, it can, the way Jason does it,' Betty answered with a chuckle. 'But there's no real harm in it, I think. Boys will be boys.'

'Was it large, Betty?'

'The fish? Yes. A real whopper.'

'My! What a little Hercules we seem to have brought into this world.'

'Hercules, Mrs Callow?'

'Yes. You must have heard of *him*, Betty – a character in Greek mythology: in Greek legend, that is.'

'Well, I have heard *about* such stories, at least. Isn't there one about a man who sleeps with his mother? – Who marries her, in fact?'

'Yes; without knowing it, of course. He is innocent of the crime he commits.'

'Well, that sounds like some old rum of a tale to me, Mrs Callow. I don't care for stories in which there is no hope of improvement. Did he have children by her? By his mother, I mean?'

'Yes.'

'Without knowing they would be his own brothers and sisters, so to speak?'

'Yes.'

'Good grief,' said Betty, with a frightened look in her eye. 'I think I'll stick to Charles Dickens.'

VI

AFTER HE HAD lingered for a while, to make sure that Arnold was asleep, Jason switched off the lights in Arnold's apartment and climbed the stairs to his own suite of rooms; that were now in darkness – or rather in near darkness; for now the silver glow of moonlight spilled in from the skies beyond his windows. And as he did so, Jason found himself reflecting upon an action he had taken just a few days before, when, without thinking of what he was doing, and in a most urgent, compulsive manner, he had purchased a pair of shiny, hard-covered notebooks.

For years, it had been Jason's habit to write down any odd thoughts he might have upon smallish scraps of paper, and then, in order to build a first draft of whatever he might be working at, to gradually transfer these notes into a series of soft-covered exercise books. So to have suddenly broken that habit, and to have bought such a different type of writing material, was an unusual action for him to take: and he was made curious by it; having learned that the things we 'do' – the actions we take – seem mostly to be governed by some subconscious form of impulse, in that we are in the main subjective creatures – who, tragically, it would seem, are limited by the fact that the conscious part of our make-up is only a fraction of our entire being.

Why, he asked himself, had he bought these two books?

For what reason was he now going to find them, as if waiting for him, placed close to the foot of his bed? Why had he not put them away? Why had he not hidden them; in some cupboard; or in a drawer?

On entering his bedroom, he swiftly crossed the room to switch on a tall, anglepoise lamp that stood close to one of the room's half-open windows; and on turning, found himself confronted by these two notebooks; lying side by side upon a chest, in which an extra pillow and a few blankets were stored.

'Why? he asked himself again, as he picked up one of the books, and as he held it respectfully in his hands – opening it with care, and looking through its off-white virginal pages.

'And why *two* of them?' he added.

The replies to his questions were to be given the following day. Not in the early part of it, when he felt lost and confused, and when he was suffering yet another fit of depression, but in the late afternoon, when the house was quiet and when a gentle breeze from the river blew in through his open windows. For it was then that he took up what he would come to think of as the 'first' of these two books – and, almost without being conscious of what he was doing, and as if he was continuing the action that had driven him to buy them, he began to write.

He had been reading – stretched out upon his bed: had got up to have a drink and to go to the lavatory: had seen the notebooks as he had re-entered the room, and had simply crossed to them, picked up one of them; sat down on the edge of his bed; stretched out to reach for a pencil that he happened to have seen on his bedside table – and then, leaning upon one elbow, had begun to set down, in the first pages of this book, a stream of thoughts: thoughts that he was now aware had been locked inside him for a very long time, and that he must find some means – some way – of releasing.

'Why?' – his narrative began with that very word, using the question as its opener – 'have I begun to write in this book? It is not my habit to write directly onto pages that are fixed; set; that are already bound. It never has been. Nor is it a habit of mine to write down anything that is in no way pre-plotted or pre-planned – anything of length, that is, and that has not been drafted in previous notes and sketches; sometimes on the backs of used envelopes; even, just once or twice, on sheets of toilet paper, when I have been out for the day, perhaps, and have had nothing with me upon which to write, and a public convenience has provided me with the quickest means of supplying such a thing. And I have quite liked that: quite enjoyed it – the use of the toilet paper, I mean. Not because of it being "for" the toilet (that sort of thing holds no meaning for me) but because the public kind is usually less soft than the domestic one. And I have taken pleasure in writing with pen, or more probably with pencil, upon its slightly shiny surface. The mind, it seems to me, has a peculiar way of working, and it is one that puzzles me. Mine certainly does, and has been puzzling me for days – no, for weeks. Why, for instance, have I not been answering my doorbell and my telephone? Why have I not rung, why have I not spoken to, my parents?; considering that I usually do – *always* do, in fact – at least once a fortnight, if not a little more. They are growing old. I am fond of them. They are fond of me. Yet for some reason, I have been unable to do it – which is stupid; and seems in some way to be immature – adolescent of me.

'When I was young – when I was a teenager, that

is, which my own children are now – I would often suffer blockages of that kind: would forget my parents' birthdays, for example – then remember them too late, and then do nothing about it. Or I would tell myself a hundred times that I should send a note to an uncle, or to an aunt, for some present that had been sent to me, yet still be unable to do it; and would be finally prompted into it by my mother; or by Betty, my parents' housekeeper, who would make me feel ashamed of myself; and that I had behaved badly – which I had, of course. But I suspect that almost everyone experiences that type of thing when they are young: a kind of tidal flow of energy that is flowing away from the exterior world with all its duties and demands; and that is carrying one – where? To some unknown destination? To a world in which one simply dreams: passes the time – wastes it, perhaps? Everyone, I am sure, has experienced that.

'But to be experiencing it *now*, that is a different story. It makes me think that I am in some way sick; ill; mentally, I mean; and the writer in me wants to know what illness it is from which I appear to be suffering, and have been suffering for weeks – perhaps for months: maybe for even more; going back for several years to – when?

'Here, my pencil pauses; hesitates; as if it had touched upon something that it cannot quite bring itself to recognise, and that it would do wrong to force. After all, I know, because I have read of it in books, that there are areas of the mind that need to be left alone; that there are mental swamps, forests, that it is unwise to disturb or to enter; and that it can be dangerous to push into or explore.

'And yet, I have to do *some*thing! The sight of myself in that mirror! The sagging flesh; the unhealthy

colour. So horrid! So horrible! The excessive drinking, eating, having made me what? – a monster? Even
my landlord, Arnold, is not that. Eccentric though he
may be, he is not a monster. I spend so much of my
time alone these days; roaming the streets; sometimes,
I notice, being glad to be physically close to people in
the shops: people I do not know and have not seen
before in my life, but the warmth of whose bodies I
experience briefly as they pass, or as they brush quickly
against me. Usually men, I notice (curious that) as if I
am seeking some lost or other part of myself.

'This is quite new to me. It is true that I have had
only a few relationships with women, but nonetheless,
my marriage was a successful one; or it was at first,
at least; and for quite some time. But then, as the
children grew, things began to change and then to
go wrong. And I didn't face it: still haven't faced it.

'They – meaning both the children and my wife,
Jill, began to – well, how shall I put it? – to offend me.
I objected to their – yes, to their very existence; and
I began to retreat from them: to withdraw, as I see it
now – meaning, as I am writing this – into myself.

'And the time feels so strange. Nothing seems to
be quite real – quite tangible; except, perhaps, for
the food that I eat. There is that moment – usually
just once a day – when, as I sit down at table (now
almost always in a restaurant, and which I am able to
afford, thank goodness, due to the money left to me
by my grandfather) I get a temporary sense of density,
of opacity; of things being solid and concrete. For the
rest of the time, I either see through things, almost
as if they were transparent, or I find myself looking
at the people and places around me as if from some
great distance.

'What disturbs me, and what has been disturbing

me this very day – and which does so almost *every* day – is that I have heard how people who have been ill – who have been extremely ill, that is – and who have been in danger of dying, will often experience this kind of sensation: of being removed from the things around them; as if, some say, they are looking down from a great height; or are peering down some great tunnel towards a glow of light at its end.

'Not that I have had the latter type of experience. Not for me is there the glow of any kind of promise lying ahead. But this much at least I am able to say; am able to acknowledge about myself; that although only just, I have at least managed to maintain a degree of presence in this world; and that the things I touch, that I fondle, that I occasionally almost kiss, still create a sweet sensation for me, that tells me I am still here: still not quite a monster: still a mortal, earthly being.

But where am I at other times? Where do I go? These are questions that nag away at my mind. And wherever it is or might be, another question I need to ask myself is why do I want to go there? – why do I find myself giving in it would appear so willingly to the peculiar kind of listlessness that leads to such departure?

'When I was young (must I go back that far?) I recall how, unlike my brother, Jeremy, who, as far as I could gather, and from the little he ever spoke about such matters, was untroubled by his body; and who always felt that he was in control of it; and that he could command it to sleep when sleep was needed; or to be bright and alert when that was what was required, I, by contrast, felt – indeed, *knew* – that my body had a force in it, a strength, that it was beyond my power to govern. Even when I was tiny – like six or seven, I mean – I felt this sense of being in some way driven by my physique: and that it could compel me into actions for which I could hardly feel responsible.

'And this is a truth about myself that I have done my best to avoid: have *never* faced, in fact, until now, this very moment. It is strange how the action of a pen, or of a pencil, can sometimes lead one to confront such a thing; but the truth will out, as they say, and so often as good a means for it happening can be the marking of a sheet of paper, such as the one upon which I am writing now, by an instrument of writing.

'Did the first scribes, when they set down upon tablets of clay their tales – their stories (their 'myths' usually; for more often than not they were tales that had formed over a considerable period of time, and that were known by a large number of people) – experience this sense of a truth coming out: of it being faced – truly faced, that is – now that the time for setting it down had finally come? And has such a time come for me – or for *my* story, rather? Not the outer one: not the outer story; which is mainly a lie. Not the one of my conformity; of how, lowering my head, as it were, and wanting to do all that was expected of me, I picked my way along on an accepted, collective course; learned, studied, did fairly well at school; was told that I could write (by my mother); believed that I could, and that I had a gift for it; got my work published when I was young (too young); married; had two children; became something (only just something) of a figure in the world of books and of words; developed a readership – a devoted one, it seems – that will always purchase the books that I write; or that will purchase my novels, at least (my one biography, which is of a poet, did very badly, I am afraid); and have attracted quite a few critics as well; who always speak nicely

– who speak decently – about my work; who always say that I am a "good" writer, and in the "upper bracket", as they put it. No, not *that* story: not the one of the appearance, as I suppose one might call it, but another one, that has to be lived on the inside – lived secretly; lived privately. Is *that* the one that I now have to face; and have to face by telling it, by setting it down – here, in this new notebook, that I bought just a few days ago; one of a pair: as if I already knew (because one *can* know such things, I believe) that what they would be used for – indeed, what they are *being* used for already – would require quite a few pages; more than just one bookful of them? And as if I knew as well that the time had at last come for putting my house – my garden – in order?

'Well, we shall see. I'll write it if I can – that other story: that inside one; that alternative one. I'll examine myself – take a good look at myself; avoid none of the warts, none of the wrinkles. Speak of fears. Speak of desires, perhaps, but not perhaps of hopes. That is a truth that I can declare on this page at once; that hope, for me, is a thing that appears to have gone out of the window, or down the drain, or the plughole, or somewhere like that. Because of what I am – meaning, because of what I have become. Because I have lived so much to suit others and not to suit myself. Because I have done all the right, all the accepted things, that a man is expected to do (including, I might add, fight for my country in the army, which my conscience told me I really ought *not* to have done), the image I have presented to the world, and that to a certain extent I have accepted and taken on, has been a *sham*.

'There! I have said something that I have avoided saying – or thinking even – for years; yet which I now know to be true, and which I have vaguely known must be true as the story of my outer life has developed. And being somewhat tired (I am writing this after having slept badly last night, due to my neighbour having fallen asleep in a chair; and to his having tumbled onto the floor; and to his having left all his lights on, as a result) I think I shall leave things for the moment.

'The beginning of any piece of writing is bound to be difficult – or it seems to be for me, at least: the strain of it being the cost on the emotions that it suggests must lie ahead. Or that certainly appears to be the case with *this* piece of writing. I am already daunted by the idea of it; by the lack of caution with which I have entered into it; by the lack of planning – of preparing; both of which have always acted for me as a kind of protection in the past, and have afforded me the conceit of believing that I was the sole master of my words.

'Now, it would seem, I have to think differently: think inwardly, shall I say. Even if the end result is a mess – something of a gabble – it won't matter, perhaps. "Meaning," said someone (I think this was in a recently published article I read about Jung – Carl Gustav Jung, that is – who now, it would seem, is taking over from Freud, as it were); "Meaning," he said, "makes a great many things endurable – perhaps everything." And I *have* to give my life some meaning, or give it a deeper one than has been given to it so far. Otherwise, I am at the end of the road, it seems to me, when, unable to continue the lie of my past existence, I shall become – what? A nonentity, I suppose. A nobody: a nothing.'

VII

THE FOLLOWING MORNING, and after he had slept particularly well, Jason decided that he must telephone his parents
to apologise for his silence; or that he must telephone his
mother, rather, since his father rarely spoke to him on
the phone. 'Caught up in a piece of work,' was the
excuse he gave her; to which he then added that he had
nonetheless been thinking about them – meaning both his
parents – a lot.

His mother expressed some of the concern she had
been experiencing, and quickly told him about his brother
coming to London that very night, and of how Jeremy
had been ringing him in the hope that they might meet
the following day.

'You don't see each other *that* often,' she had said, 'and I
think Jeremy has been concerned about you; as I have been;
as, indeed, we *all* have been. So why don't you call him,
Jason? He'll be in town for only a few days – staying with
friends in Victoria; so not far from you. At the Addisons',
Polly's godparents. Do you remember them? I'll give you
their number.'

Jason took the number and assured his mother that he
would ring her again soon, and before long would come
to visit her. Then he determined that he would contact
Jeremy later that day at the Addisons', and would attempt
to arrange a meeting. Not that he had any really strong

desire to see his brother. Fond of him though he was, they had grown apart in recent years; for although Jeremy had appeared to be sympathetic regarding the break-up of Jason's marriage, Jason had the impression that both Jeremy and his wife, Helen, had in some way disapproved of what had happened – even though it had been Jill, Jason's wife, who had gone off to live in Cumbria with her mother, and who had taken the children with her.

However, Jeremy was his brother, and there was a bond between them that had been forged in childhood; and that allowed them to go for months without seeing each other; or without even speaking to each other on the telephone – even once, for almost a year – and yet still know that when they did finally meet or speak, there would be no real awkwardness between them.

Jason next turned his thoughts away from Jeremy and towards his landlord. He had rung Arnold earlier in the day to make sure that he was all right, and had noticed that his speech was a little slurred; and although Arnold had quickly assured him that it was due only to his having drunk too much the previous night, Jason felt that he should now go down and call at his door, rather than just speak to him again on the telephone: telling himself that Arnold was both proud and clever-minded, and that he might have been able to disguise from him on the phone that he was more seriously unwell.

However, whatever the cause of it had been, there was no sign of Arnold's speech being slurred when Jason called to see him that evening, at about six; and after he had written that first entry in his new notebook. For Arnold was now looking quite sprightly, and insisted upon Jason joining him for a drink. 'There's wine,' he said. 'Or port, dear, if you would prefer it,' he had added; knowing that Jason was particular about such things, and that the port he was able to offer was of a less inferior quality.

'You will stay for a bit – won't you?' Arnold had then half pleaded; always being glad of any form of company; and at any time of the day or, indeed, of the night.

'Here. I'll move these,' he said, as he lifted a stack of newspapers out of a chair and placed them upon the floor beside another. 'It's a real honour, you know,' he added teasingly. 'We don't get to see you here that often.'

Jason sat, and Arnold went off to fetch the port, leaving Jason relieved to know that nothing appeared to be wrong, and that life could now go on again as a normal. Or not quite as normal, in that the notebooks he had just bought had wrought such a change in his life. For suddenly he had a cause; an interest; and it was an intense one; and one that had already begun to release him from some of the blockages he had been suffering; enabling him to ring his parents, for example, and to be determined to ring his brother later, and perhaps see him the following day. For he could now understand that doing these things would in no way bind him or inhibit him. On the contrary, they would allow him the liberty that he needed in order to write; and to write about himself for once; and to say the things that he now felt sure he needed to say, and that so urgently needed saying.

'Well,' said Arnold, as he returned with a bottle of port in one hand and a pair of small, quite delicate wineglasses in the other, 'this *is* a treat. Tell me, Jason, how are you? You seem to be less grumpy than you were; than you have been of late. Has something happened?'

Jason smiled, feeling for once some kind of real affection for his landlord; and some admiration for him as well, in that he had so quickly sensed that there had been a change in him, and that he was now feeling different from how he had felt for the past few weeks.

'Oh, nothing important,' answered Jason, knowing that

Arnold always looked for outer changes, rather than inner ones, and thinking that he had probably already made up his mind that the change he saw in Jason was due to his having had some kind of affair: 'I've been working, Arnold – that's all; and I am glad of it.'

'Oh, well, yes – of *course* you are. You're an artist, aren't you? Artists are only happy when they're at work, poor things. I've never been one myself – though I would have liked to have been. I'm not creative in that sense. I never was. But I've known artists all my life, you see; mostly in the cinema – and in the theatre too, of course; and I've seen how very unstable they can be, and how it is only their work that really steadies them.'

Jason reflected upon this, wondering if it was entirely true; but knowing that it certainly seemed to be true enough about him at that moment. For although he was glad to be able to be polite and civilised with Arnold for a change, and to be able to spend a little time with him, his mind had now become half fixed upon what he had been writing that afternoon; upon that line – that inner narrative – that he had just begun to release; and that was making him think of a passage that he had once read in Proust (and that he must now look up, he kept telling himself, when he went upstairs to his rooms); about an artist not being free, and that what he has to do is to 'discover' what he is creating; as if it were pre-existent to him, and as if it might be a law of nature.

'Well; now that you've come down for once, wouldn't you like to join us for the evening?' Arnold then asked. 'I'm having a little party, you see – late. Lottie – you know my friend Lottie, Jason, don't you? – she's going to be here; and the boys too, of course – John and Billy. And Sophie as well. Do you know her, Jason? "Miss Nondescript" we call her.'

Jason thanked him but said no, giving as his excuse the

fact that his brother was about to arrive in London, and that there was the chance he might be seeing him; even though he was sure they wouldn't meet until the next day.

'Oh, your brother – yes. That's Jeremy, isn't it? You've spoken about him before. In fact, hasn't he been *here* once; to see you at the house? Called here, I mean?'

'He has,' answered Jason.

'Or more than once, I think,' Arnold added, always wanting to know as much as he could of other people's affairs.

'Several times,' said Jason.

'Oh – *is* it?' said Arnold, lowering his eyes for a moment, then suddenly raising them again. 'Tell me, dear – is he good-looking?'

Jason laughed. 'Good-looking? Yes. I suppose he is.'

'Better than you, Jason, I mean?' said Arnold with a wry smile.

'Oh, *I'm* not good-looking,' answered Jason, laughing a second time. 'I wish I was, Arnold.'

'Well, you're good-looking enough for me, dear,' Arnold replied, turning his questioning into a flirt. 'Really good-looking men are a bore, you know. They only have time for themselves. All the girls know that . . . Now, Jason, have another glass. Port is good for you.'

This time Jason declined; and after a few more exchanges of chatter, he left; thinking to himself that he would first go out to have a bite to eat, and then speak to his brother on his return – assuming that Jeremy would have arrived at the Addisons' by then, and wondering whether he would be different; and what exactly they might speak about when they met, other than the usual brotherly talk, and the spread of family gossip that always goes with it.

At ten o'clock that night, Arnold began to prepare for his little 'gathering', knowing that none of his guests would be arriving before ten-thirty or gone; except Lottie, perhaps, who was usually early; but whose presence was always welcome, since she was so neat and tidy in her ways, and would arrange the table for him with care.

'I've got in a piece of Dolcelatte, for a change,' Arnold would tell her when she arrived, which was a great treat in those days, when the shops as yet weren't flooded with continental delicacies.

'Oh, I don't like it,' said Lottie flatly. 'Give me a good old piece of English cheese any day. Like Stilton, I mean. It's the best there is in the world. Most English things are. I don't know why there should be all this clamour for stuff from abroad.'

'Well, there's no Stilton for you tonight, darling,' Arnold told her. 'You'll have to make do with Cheddar.'

'Is it a good one?' asked Lottie, as she set out a number of plates and glasses upon the lace-edged cloth that Arnold had just spread over a table top.

'It's just Cheddar, dear,' answered Arnold, a little sharply. 'Whether it's good or not doesn't come into it.'

Lottie ignored this remark, as she ignored so much of what Arnold would say. And, on turning to a mirror, occupied herself with checking to see that her make-up was in order.

'Lottie. Do you know who came to see me today?' asked Arnold.

'God knows. The Queen, I suppose.'

'No.'

'Princess Margaret, then.'

'*No* – silly! Someone local. Someone we were speaking about only yesterday.'

'Oh! Your neighbour, you mean. The writer. Why did *he* come to see you?'

'Just to make sure that I was all right – that's all. Very

kind of him, I thought. He seemed different. Different from how he has been of late, that is.'

'In what way?'

'Well – I don't know. More human, perhaps: or something. More present.'

'Not drunk then, I presume.'

'No! He's *never* drunk, Lottie. He drinks a lot, but he's never drunk.'

'They're the worst kind,' remarked Lottie firmly, as if she might be an authority on the subject. 'The silent types, as they call them . . . Arnold, is this eyelash of mine coming *off*, or is it just my imagination?'

'Oh, you fusspot, you. Always going on about your clothes and about your looks. Of *course* it's not coming off. It's too bloody big – *that's* what it is; and you're not used to them, darling. They make you look like a blinking mummy.'

'Oh, shut up,' answered Lottie. 'See to the drinks. I've done all the glasses for you; rubbed all of them clean. And you do know that Darren is coming, don't you, Arnold? John and Billy's friend: the actor, that is . . . You've not yet met him – have you? I don't like him too much, but it'll be a change. We'll have to watch what we say though. Mind our gossip a little. Walls have ears, you know, when there are new people around.'

'What do you think, Lottie?' asked Arnold, who was now taking out some bottles of wine from beneath the draped table upon which the plates and glasses had been arranged. 'Shall I put out just three bottles, or four?'

'Oh, *three* won't be enough – not for six of us,' said Lottie. 'Sophie drinks like a fish, and the boys can knock back a few as well. I don't know about Darren.'

'Well, I'll put out four then,' said Arnold, who was always quick to be influenced by his friend, 'and if someone brings me a bottle, I'll just swap theirs for one of mine.'

And it was as Arnold said this that they heard a sharp

ring on the doorbell and guessed that their party was about to begin.

'Lottie, dear – go down and let them in, if you will. It'll be Sophie, I expect. I don't know if that Darren is going to be with them, but the boys don't leave the theatre until ten-thirty, I think they said. And they've got their own key in any case.'

Lottie flicked her fingers and glanced swiftly into the mirror again; then went out and down the stairs; feeling quite pleased with herself and with her appearance. But on opening the main entrance-door of the house she received a shock; for standing there, with blood streaming down his forehead, was Jason.

'Arnold!' shrieked Lottie, unable to stand the sight of blood, and having retreated into the hallway and then run back to the foot of the staircase.

'Arnold!' she shrieked a second time, with a look of real horror on her face.

'Lottie, dear, whatever *is* it?' Arnold's voice responded, as he moved with surprising speed, padding in slippered feet onto the landing.

'Arnold! It's your neighbour. It's Mister –'

'Callow,' muttered Jason from beneath lowered eyebrows, and as he stumbled through the open doorway, feeling that he might be about to faint.

'Jason!' cried Arnold, seeing the blood that Jason was now wiping from his forehead. 'What *have* you done? . . . Lottie! Quickly! Come! Ring for a doctor – for *my* doctor. His number's on a card close to the telephone.'

Lottie obeyed, being glad to escape the scene; and fearing that she might be asked to apply first-aid or something; any form of nursing care being beyond her. And as she went up, Arnold came down; picking his way with caution, but still moving at surprising speed.

'John! Billy!' Arnold then cried, as he reached the foot of the staircase, and as he saw the two of them step in through the open doorway. 'Quickly! Come! We need your help.'

But before John and Billy could adjust to what was happening, Jason had collapsed, and lay in a heap upon the floor.

'John! Help me lift him,' cried Billy.

'He's not broken anything, has he?' John asked Arnold, as he dashed across to Billy.

'We'll just get him to the stairs,' Billy then said, not waiting to hear Arnold's reply; 'where he can sit;' which they did; and where Jason half recovered consciousness; enough to mutter something to Arnold about his brother being in town, and to hand him a crumpled sheet of paper upon which he had written the telephone number of the Addisons', which his mother had given to him that morning.

'We've sent for a doctor, Jason,' said Arnold.

'But we'd still do well to clean that wound, I think,' said Billy, who was good at such things, and who had now taken out his own handkerchief, which was unused, and had applied it to Jason's forehead.

'Do you have proper stuff for that?' John asked Arnold. 'First-aid stuff, I mean.'

'There's a box in my bathroom,' Arnold replied, 'next to the mirror . . . And it's clearly *marked*!' he shouted, as John raced up the stairs.

And so it was that by the time the doctor had arrived, Jason's wound had been bathed and dressed, and it had become obvious to everyone that, severe though it was, it wasn't all that deep a cut – more of nasty graze; but with heavy bruising, which the doctor later confirmed. And after a while, when he felt sufficiently composed and had sufficiently recovered from the shock, Jason insisted upon climbing the stairs to his rooms; which he did slowly, and with John and Billy's help.

'Oh, dear,' said Arnold to Lottie, who was standing close to him on the landing, watching the three figures ascend, 'you never know what's going to happen in life, do you? . . . Now, Lottie dear, I think I'd better ring and tell his brother. Certainly, someone in the family ought to be told; in case it's something worse than we've been thinking . . . Come now. Let's have a drink. The boys will see to it all. I'll just give his brother a call and it'll be off our hands for the moment.'

Jason slept for more than an hour, then half woke, hearing the muted sounds of voices below, and at the same time becoming conscious of the fact that there was someone sitting close to him on his bed.

'Jason?' he heard a voice say, 'it's me. It's Jeremy.'

'Jeremy?' replied Jason quietly, not opening his eyes. 'How? What happened?'

'You must have fallen; or slipped or something – in the street. A doctor has been. You spoke to him, I gather. He said it's nothing too serious, thank goodness; although it will be wise, he thinks, to have it looked at in the morning.'

'Ah,' said Jason, still partly dazed, but now opening his eyes. 'And how do *you* come to be here, Jeremy? – to know about it?'

'Your landlord. He rang me at the Addisons'. I had just arrived.'

'Ah,' said Jason a second time: then muttered to himself, 'So stupid. So utterly stupid of me.'

'Jason – don't think about it,' said his brother. 'Go back to sleep now – there's a good chap. I gather your landlord has people in – a small party; but he told me that he'd get rid of them early, and asked me to assure you of that.'

'Ah,' replied Jason, yet another time, not quite taking in what his brother had said.

'Look, Jason,' said Jeremy, 'I've got to go. I've been here for well over an hour. I'll ring you in the morning. Or better, I'll just turn up here at about ten, when the doctor is due . . . Now,' he said, lightly patting his brother's thigh, 'you just rest – do you hear? You've had a nasty blow. You weren't coshed, I hope. It was a fall, Jason – wasn't it?'

Jason smiled. 'Thanks, Jeremy,' was all he replied.

'Right then. I'll be off,' said Jeremy, 'and I'll be back to see you tomorrow . . . Take it easy now; and if you *do* need anything, your landlord said that all you have to do is to knock on the floor; if you can't get to the telephone, that is.'

Jason smiled again, which Jeremy didn't quite understand; not knowing that what Jason's mind was now directed towards was the contents of his new notebooks; that were lying in wait for him, as it were. And that what he would be using them for was the setting down of a few truths: and that nothing – not even the sudden diversion of this accident – could prevent him from fulfilling that idea.

'Goodnight,' Jeremy called out, as he was about to leave; and as John appeared at the doorway; who had come to make sure that Jason was all right.

'Goodnight,' answered Jason; for the first time looking his brother directly in the face, and taking in how very well he appeared to be, and how trim and neat and clean-looking; and all the things that he believed that he was not.

It is of no real consequence to the narrative of this book to know exactly what the cause of Jason's accident had been

– which is just as well, probably, since he seemed intent upon telling it to no one; not even to the doctor when he came to see him the following day: and he would reply to any suggestions that he had perhaps tripped or stumbled in the street with a 'possibly', or an 'I expect so.'

However, what *is* of importance to the narrative of this book, is to realise that, to Jason's mind, all this seemed part of some scheme, and of the changes that were being wrought in his life. Not in his outer life, or in his daily life, for that was little different from how it had always been (in recent years, that is), in that he hadn't changed his habits much, or met someone new, with whom he had become involved, or to whom he had become attached. But in his inner life; in the life of what we now call the psyche and that used to be called the soul. For he had the feeling – indeed, he had the knowledge – that he was being forced by pressures that were beyond his control, to release thoughts and ideas that were deep, and that he had not touched upon before; and that had been held in check for years – perhaps for all his life. And he felt excited by this, sensing, as he did, that there was danger in it. Danger, that is, in the way that one would sense danger if one were about to release a wild animal from a cage; knowing that it could lead to one's death, perhaps, or to some savage form of wounding; and yet being conscious, at the same time, that this was a risk he wanted to take: that for some reason, this seemed to be a *necessary* form of action, and one which, if it became thwarted or suppressed, could bring death to him of a different kind. A death of the spirit, that is, that roots itself in secrecy and lies; and that puts truth on hold; forcing it to wait for its release until some other point in time; and which was something at which, over the years, Jason had become skilled.

Within minutes of his brother having left the room, and

75

of his having given strong assurances to John that he was comfortable, and that all he was wanting to do was to sleep, Jason had crawled his way to the foot of his bed, in order to collect the 'first' of his two notebooks: then he had picked up a pencil with which to write, and had switched on a light close to his pillow.

'I will *not* tell lies,' he hurriedly set down – abandoning all habits he had of neatness. 'Not any longer. Tomorrow, if I can – if I am well enough; or if not that, then the day after, or the day after that again; I will attempt to pursue this line, wher*ever* it might be leading me. *This*' (he underlined the word heavily) 'is a promise I now make myself, and it is one that I vow to keep.'

VIII

IT WAS A week later that Jason's painter-friend, Joseph Mallory, decided that he was going to pay Jason a visit in order to find out how he was; not having been satisfied by what had been said to him on the telephone when Jason had spoken about his accident, and when Jason had refused to meet him out at their local pub.

Or that was the reason Joseph had given himself for calling; perhaps a deeper one being that he was feeling an urgent need to express himself, and to speak to Jason about his latest ideas (this time, regarding the theatre) and for which he needed Jason as a good listener. In the meantime — meaning, during the week that had just passed — one of the big surprises of Jason's life had been the quick relationship that had developed between himself and John and Billy; for they were the ones, not Arnold, who had decided to make themselves responsible for him; taking over from Jason's brother, Jeremy, as it were: who was in London for only a few days; and who had little time to spare in any case.

At first, Jason had been startled by the intensity of John and Billy's concern, since it was something with which he was unfamiliar (in men, that is), and that he couldn't quite understand: the fuss they made over him having been prompted to an extent by the slight disgust they had first felt regarding his lack of domesticity; and by the general disorder of his rooms: the clothes that were strewn here and there: the books that were stacked so messily in bookcases and against walls, and that were piled high and close to the ceilings.

'And he can't even fry a bloody egg,' Billy had said one night to John, when they were snuggled up together in bed; and after they had been to visit Jason and had taken him some food.

'Well, neither can I,' replied John.

'Oh, yes you *can*; or you could if you *had* to,' protested Billy.

'If I *had* to, yes. I suppose I could.'

'Of *course* you could. Besides, you can do a lot of other things; like peeling spuds, for instance; or emptying dustbins; and – well, lots of things. Painting and decorating too. You painted the bathroom. That's more than I can do. *And* you're tidy – that's the important thing. I hate men who aren't orderly. And his bloody kitchen smells – did you notice it? It's not been cleaned for weeks, I should think. I'll have to have a go at it in the morning.'

'Or *I* will,' said John.

'Well, you will then. One of us will.'

For which type of reason, John and Billy were often at Jason's flat: never calling unannounced (they were sensitive about things like that), but saying to him when they left that they would be back to see him the following day, or the day after perhaps; and at what time; and not taking a no from Jason as an answer.

'We'll do it until you're better,' said John. 'Until you are well enough. We like you – don't we, Billy? – we *want* to do it.'

As they prepared food for him, and as they cleaned and tidied his rooms, Jason regarded his new friends in astonishment; appreciating the fact that they never disturbed his books; or, if they were forced to move them, always putting them back carefully where they had found them once they were clean.

Did he really need them? Jason wondered, when, within a few days of his accident, he was at least well enough to be up and about, if not as yet to leave the house; and when he believed that he could quite easily have managed on his own, had he just called on some of his friends; including Joseph, of course, who had missed seeing him, and who would have been more than pleased to help.

'Now, Jason,' Joseph said when he arrived, 'tell me. What happened? Come on. Tell me. Did you fall, Jason? Were you drunk? Did someone have a go at you, or what?'

'I really don't know,' replied Jason, with a smile that almost became a smirk. 'Fell, probably . . . But I wasn't drunk, Joe,' he asserted.

'Anyway, you seem right enough now. Who's been looking after you?'

'Friends of mine. New ones. John and Billy.'

'John and Billy? Who the fuck are *they*? I've never heard of them. Who *are* they? What do they do?'

'One's an actor – or would like to be.'

'Oh, yes, well – speaking about acting, Jason, I've been thinking about that – or about the stage, rather. All this balls there is at the moment about Bertolt Brecht – the German playwright. Have you heard of him, Jason? Very political, apparently. Very left-wing. There's a lot of talk about bringing him over here, you know – or bringing his company here, that is. It's going to revolutionise the British stage, is the claim being made – which is probably rubbish. I mean, I don't think the theatre is really a place for politics – do you? I mean, it's got to be about deeper things, more inner things than that; as the Greeks bloody well knew . . . By the way, Jason, those two blokes: those two new friends of yours; are they a couple of queers; a couple of fairies?'

79

'I really don't know,' replied Jason. 'Perhaps.'

'Oh, it's "perhaps" with you with *every* bloody thing right now, isn't it, Jason? You ever *been* with a man, Jason? – sexually, I mean.'

There was a pause before Jason answered this: then he said, looking his friend directly in the eye, 'No. Not willingly. Not voluntarily.'

'What do you bloody well *mean*, for Christ's sake – not *vol*untarily? Do you mean you were raped or something?'

'Something like that. More the other way round.'

'You mean *you* raped *some*one?'

'Yes.'

'When you were young?'

'Yes.'

'At school, you mean.'

'Yes.'

'Someone younger than yourself?'

'No. The same age: the same class. I didn't *want* to do it. I hadn't thought of doing it: hadn't planned to do it, or anything like that. It just happened – suddenly; after rugby; after a shower.'

'Well, I'll be damned. But you found out then that you weren't that way inclined, I suppose.'

'Yes – more or less.'

'Well, thank God for that. I'm never comfortable with them, you know – with queers. They make me feel uneasy. I don't know why.'

'But you would be comfortable with these, Joe . . . I'm pretty sure you would. Anyway, we're going to find out; if they continue coming here, that is.'

No sooner had Joseph left, than Jason decided that he would record their conversation in his new notebook. Not all of it. Not Joseph's comments regarding the theatre and Bertolt Brecht, but what he himself had said to Joseph about his personal life – meaning his sexual life – which was a secret he had shared before with no one. Not that he was particularly ashamed of it. To him, this was simply a buried experience of his childhood that he had chosen to keep hidden; something that anyone might have experienced when they were young, and that had simply been a part of his growing up and of the thrusts of his growing body. But precisely because of that – because it had to do with things of the body – Jason believed that it must be a part of his new story: the one that he needed to tell: a part of his other life, that is, that had been unrecognised, untold. To which he then chose to add, taking a sudden risk with himself (for he was aware of the danger of such namings) the recollection of other compulsive urges that were more sadistic in their character, and that were more difficult for him to write down; such as the compulsion he had had regarding animals, and the driving need he had felt at times to kill them: one such example being the delight he had taken (he felt there was no other word that he could use for this) in the sight of a fish he had caught, and that he had battered to death with a stone; and which had been a ritual he had indulged in quite frequently as a child. Also countless beetles and spiders that had been kept prisoner by him in matchboxes, and that had also remained as a secret of his, as he had watched them slowly starve to death. As well as the one occasion (this was something even more painful for him to set down) when, at the age of just nine or ten, he had cornered a dormouse in his parents' house in Hampshire; that had looked up at him in an almost pleading fashion; but which, on the grounds that a mousetrap had been set for it in any case, and that it was therefore destined for an unexpected death, he had picked up by the tail and then half decapitated, before plunging it into water, to watch its final struggle until it had drowned.

All this he wrote down; determined that the figure he had encountered in the mirror, and that had given him the new outer view he now had of himself, should be given an inner picture to match. How, he asked himself, could this new picture – this new view of himself, that he was now forming in his mind; this monstrous one, if you like – fit with the cool hardness of his novels, that were so controlled; so carefully wrought; so intellectual in their way? Not because of their ideas or their thought (for he never expressed any overt form of philosophy in his writings), but because of their general air of impersonality, which he knew had been a part of their success. Civilised, they were called. Fine, modern pieces of writing, they were said to be. 'What lies my books have been,' Jason wrote down. 'And how in need of lies must they have been – the people who have bought them and have read them, and who have therefore subscribed to what I have done.'

Lillian Callow believed that she had been right to feel concern for her favourite son. He had said nothing to her about his fall – or about his accident, rather; and on the grounds that she would have 'fussed, fretted, come down here and bothered me', he had convinced his brother to say nothing about it as well. But in spite of that, and in spite of the fact that they were now speaking to each other regularly on the telephone, instinct told her that something big was taking place in Jason's life: that some great upheaval was going on that made her nervous, and that at times invaded her mind. When she might be working in the garden, for example, and the late August sun might be beating down upon her back, she would suddenly feel cold, as if some cloud or shadow had passed over her; and she would then feel a need to look around her in order to see if someone had been watching her; from a distance; and which there never had been, of course; the world about her being no different from how it had ever been, with the huge cedar tree, that stood at the centre of the lawn, still swooping towards the earth in the same series of large, generous gestures; and her friend the robin (which is how she always thought of it) still picking away at the crumbs and nuts that she had thrown out for it that morning; and with the windows of the drawing-room as wide open as ever, and as welcoming as they had ever been.

'Have you heard from Jason?' Betty asked one day, and at a moment when Lilian was least expecting the question.

'No, Betty. Why? Not since Wednesday, if that is what you mean.'

'Well, I didn't exactly mean *that*, Mrs Callow. I wasn't thinking about how long it might be since you last spoke to him. It's just something I'm feeling inside me, I suppose. But I do get anxious at times when I think of him. For what reason, I do not know.'

Lilian voiced her own anxiety, glad to be able to externalise what she was feeling, but neither she nor Betty seemed able to define what might be the cause of their concern.

'It's all nonsense, I expect,' said Lilian.

'Probably,' said Betty.

'Anyway, the children will be down from Cumbria soon,' said Lilian.

'Yes; and Jill will be with them for once – won't she?' said Betty. 'It's some time now since they were all here together.'

'A long time,' said Lilian.

If Arnold's little late-night gathering had been a flop – the one that had been held in Arnold's apartment on the night of Jason's accident – it hadn't been entirely due to the high drama of the occasion; to the sight of Jason's bleeding head, or to the urgent need there had been of calling for the doctor; it had also been due to the fact that John and Billy's friend, Darren, had unfortunately failed to turn up.

'And it's very rude of him,' said Arnold, who had been looking forward to meeting someone new. 'Don't you think so, Lottie? You don't say you'll come to something – do you? – and then simply not show up.'

'He's like that,' said Billy sharply, speaking in Darren's defence.

'Then why do you want to be friendly with him, Billy, if this is typical of his behaviour? . . . Think of all the bother I've gone to,' he went on, 'getting all *this* prepared.'

Billy felt like saying that the amount of food on the table that evening hardly warranted such a description; and thought of the quick fry-up he and John would be in need of when they got home.

'He's an actor,' said Lottie, speaking of Darren; and as if that might end the conversation.

'Yes – well – so is Billy,' said Arnold, 'or he's *trying* to be one; aren't you, Billy? But he doesn't do *that*, Lottie. Doesn't accept to come to a party; then simply not turn up for it.'

Billy said nothing.

'Well, does he, John?' asked Arnold.

'Of *course* he doesn't,' said John, looking at Billy with loving eyes, and thinking to himself that he was beginning to wish that he was at home with him and in bed.

'Perhaps it's just as well,' said Sophie – Miss Nondescript, as Arnold called her, the woman with the smudged face and the straggle of greying, yellowish hair – 'what with all the upset there's been, it's just as well, probably, that he *didn't* come: this Dorren, or whatever he's called.'

'Darren,' said Billy.

'Darren then,' said Sophie.

'Darren what?' asked Lottie, not being really interested

in the talk, but needing to have something to speak about as she was seeing to one of her nails.

'Fawcett,' said Billy.

'Doesn't that mean tap?' asked Lottie, screwing up her nose.

'With a "u" it does,' said Billy. '*Then* it means tap. But this is with a "w", and there are two "t"s at the end.'

'Oh, it's double "t", is it?' said Lottie.

'Yes,' said Billy.

In those days just after the war, the streets of Chelsea were less well lit than they are today. There weren't any of those soaring street-lamps that there are now, whose stooping heads cast such a blast of light upon the traffic. Then, all was softness and shadow, with only the somewhat brighter lights of the pedestrian crossings creating a focus here and there. And in the less important streets – in the ones that lead down to the river, for example, and therefore in the one in which Jason lived – there were still a few of those really old-fashioned, box-headed lamps, that were fuelled by gas, rather than electricity; some of which, as one recalls, still needed a lamplighter to ignite them. Nor were there any of the fashionable clothes-shops, that have become such a feature of the King's Road. There was a Woolworths, of course, as there used to be then in almost every major High Street; and there was a greengrocer's, whose wares spilled onto the pavement, sheltered by an enormous, sagging awning. There was also a bookshop, and a paint-shop that is still there; and that sells materials used by artists; as well as a small, very good bakery, and an equally excellent butcher's. Which means that the area was much quieter than it is now, and more parochial. Not sleepy, exactly, for well-known artists (well-known painters) have always lived in that part of the city; as well as writers and theatricals, who have given the place much of its character and charm. But the days of the 'boutique' and of Mary Quant were yet to come. In fact, Jason's habit of meeting his painter-friend, Joe, in the bar of a local pub and of then arguing with him vociferously about the latest trends in artistic fashion, was very typical of that time. For in one particular bar on the river, the painter, Francis Bacon, and other less famous painters, such as John Minton, were to be seen doing the same thing.

Also, there was only a small number of restaurants in Chelsea in those days. There were no pizza-bars; no 'trattorias' and the like. There was one Chinese restaurant, that seemed to have been there since forever; and food was available, of course, in all the bars of the public houses (of which there were, and still are, quite a few), but usually only at lunchtimes. And there was also the new fashion then for coffee bars, as they were called, where people would often linger into the early hours; and most of which seemed to be lit dimly by lamps that were hung low over the tables, and whose shades were fashioned either from cane or from straw. And there was one such coffee bar that had been painted to look like what perhaps was the Bay of Naples, with views of the Italian coastline decorating its walls; and with white, mock-marble table tops and a chequered black and white floor.

Then, towards the eastern end of the King's Road – the end of it that is closest to Sloane Square – there was a shop that specialised in freshly-roasted coffee beans; and that had a smallish room at the back where delicious cups of coffee were served; together with a few sandwiches, and certainly with an assortment of cakes and Danish pastries, that were displayed on a chromium trolley.

This coffee shop-cum-coffee bar was all in brown veneers and brass. Brown seats, brown table tops; and behind counters at the front of the shop, large, brass-banded canisters in which the coffee beans were stored. And it was here that quite a number of the local intelligentsia, as one might speak of them, would gather. Both in the evenings and throughout the day, there would be a continual flow of people, using it as a meeting-place for their friends; arguing, smoking, gossiping, drinking coffee. Not the sort of place that Joseph Mallory would ever use; beer, not coffee, being his idea of refreshment. Nor was it a place that Jason went to very often. But there were just the odd occasions when he did. Never with someone. Always on his own; and seldom speaking to anyone either. But it was there one day, and at about three-thirty in the afternoon, and not many days before his last birthday, and therefore prior to that last visit to his parents, that Jason met someone – or encountered someone, might be a better way of describing it – who, without his being conscious of it at all (in that there was nothing to suggest that it would happen), would play a part in his life later on.

When Jason arrived, the little restaurant had been crowded, and there had been just one vacant table for two; at which Jason had sat. Then, within a few seconds of his having ordered himself a coffee, a young man sat down opposite him and dropped a shoulder-bag onto the floor.

'You don't mind,' the young man said. Not asking: simply assuming that he had a right to be there; and to be sitting down; and to be joining Jason at his table.

Jason felt annoyed by this. He disliked the young man's assertiveness; and (although he was less conscious of this) he disliked the fact that, from the very moment he had arrived, and had decided that he would sit down at Jason's table, he had taken no notice of him, of Jason, whatsoever. *And*, moreover, had immediately flicked his fingers at a waitress – who, to Jason's astonishment, considering that the place was so very busy, had responded to him at once, and had come forward to take his order. *Also*, because no sooner had he done this, than the young man picked up his bag; opened it and peered into it; then quickly pulled out a noticeably large address-book, and began to finger through its pages. Not in a very purposeful manner, but more in a restless fashion, as if he was hoping that someone's name and address might strike him as being particularly interesting or worthwhile; and as if he was looking for something by chance; something he felt a need of, but that he hadn't yet discovered.

And yet, if he felt irritated, Jason also felt drawn. Slyly, as the pages of the address-book were being turned, and as the two of them sat waiting for their coffee, Jason glanced across the table, wondering who this young man might be, and what he might do for a living; noticing that his dark, auburnish hair, that was not dissimilar in colour to his own, was cut quite short; and noting as well that his skin was sallow; and that he was thin, but not gaunt; and that he had eyes that were either very dark brown or black (they were moving too rapidly for Jason to be sure); and also long, fine fingers and clean, freshly trimmed nails.

'Your coffee, sir,' the waitress said to Jason, lowering a cup and saucer in front of him . . . 'And yours, sir,' she said to the young man, with a bright smile.

'Thank you,' the young man answered, looking up at her quickly and making some kind of instantaneous contact with her, but certainly not of a sexual kind.

'Did you want something to eat, sir?' she asked. 'A pastry or something?'

The young man's eyes became still for a second, and Jason saw that there were bluish tinges in their highlights, that gave the pupils extra depth.

'No, thank you,' he answered graciously . . . 'No thanks,' he then repeated, as he turned back to the pages of his address-book.

'And you, sir?' the waitress then said to Jason.

'Me, what?' asked Jason grumpily – almost offensively.

'Do you need anything else, sir?' the waitress said to him coldly, 'anything to eat, sir. A pastry or something?'

'Oh – no . . . No, thank you,' said Jason, realising that he had been impolite. 'Just the coffee . . . Thank you.'

Neither Jason nor the young man spoke to each other; and Jason felt sure that the young man hadn't really looked at him – hadn't really taken him in: that is, until the moment when he (meaning Jason) rose to leave, and when he asked the waitress for his bill. For then the young man suddenly said to him, 'Is it always like this?'

'I beg your pardon,' answered Jason, caught out; and not quite knowing what the young man had meant.

'This bar – this restaurant. Is it always as crowded? As this, I mean?'

'Oh – yes . . . It is . . . *Always*,' said Jason with a grunt, and as he turned on his heels and left.

IX

'LILIAN, DEAR; ARE you fretting about something?'

'Why do you ask, Edgar? Do I appear to be?'

'Yes. You do. I have noticed it . . . It has nothing to do with Jason, I hope.'

'Yes, Edgar. I'm afraid that it has.'

'But I thought all was well again now; that he'd just been busy – writing or something; but is now speaking to us again regularly. Which he is – isn't he? The same as he has always done?'

'I know, Edgar, but –'

'But what, Lilian?'

'But I'm not *happy*. There is something wrong, Edgar – going on – that I don't know about. Instinct tells me this.'

'Instinct, oh, is that what it is? If I were you, Lilian, I'd be suspicious of that. You aren't ill – are you? You aren't projecting onto Jason troubles that are your own?'

'No, Edgar, I am not. For my age, I count myself fit. And you shouldn't sneer at instinct, you know. It sees things that are hidden.'

'Oh, is that what it does? Well, it's beyond me – *that* type of thing. I trust in thought, Lilian, and reason. I have relied on them all my life. It's not Betty who has put these ideas into your head, I hope.'

'No, Edgar. Betty and I just feel the same way. It is not

ideas that we have put into each others' head. She believes, as I do, that Jason is – well, we don't know what; but we both feel that something is amiss.'

'Well, if you don't know why, or what it is, and if it's all guesswork, I hardly think it worth talking about. To my mind, you should face troubles only when they come to you – not go looking for them.'

'I think, Edgar,' said Lilian firmly, 'that we had better speak no more about this . . . Now, what about tea? Shall we have it here, out in the garden? Or would you prefer to have it indoors?'

Edgar Callow looked at his wife in the hope of under-standing her 'condition', as he had already named it in his mind; but all he could see was that she was in some way not herself, and he felt irritated by it.

'I think we'll have it indoors,' he replied a little tetchily, 'if you don't mind . . . I have a book to finish and the wind prevents me from concentrating. Would you like me to go and tell Betty?'

'No, dear – *I* will. If you would just put away these things for me – this trowel: this basket. Betty must be asleep, or reading, perhaps. You know how she is, once she gets lost in a book. She's like you, Edgar. She has no room or time for anyone.'

Edgar Callow smiled.

'Oh, dear, Lilian,' he said. 'What you have to put up with, having two readers in the house.'

'Yes. But I do have *this*,' said Lilian, speaking of her garden, and as she left her husband to go inside the house to find Betty, and as she looked around her with pride at what she saw as the beauty of such tidiness and order.

*

'And it is *always* beautiful here,' stated Jason, reflecting

91

Lilian's thoughts about her garden, and as he sat opposite her in a deckchair during his first visit since his accident.

'I never tire of it,' his mother replied. 'It *is* a lot of work; but more than worth it, I think. And I do have Gordon, you know, who now comes here twice a week.'

Jason gave no reply to this. He was so enjoying himself; just being there – just sitting there, on such a warm September day; and feeling, as he so often did, that the countryside could heal him in some way and give him the rest and comfort that he needed.

His mother looked at him, as he sat half facing her, quite close to her, and with his features partly in shadow: and with what she now saw as the over-large bulk of his presence seeming almost to threaten her.

Was this the son she knew? she wondered: the one who had always meant so very much to her, and who had always seemed to match her idea of what a son of hers should be? Why, she asked herself, did he no longer appear to reflect that idea? He had never dressed tidily, but with his being a writer – an artist – she had always accepted, rather than objected to, a degree of slovenliness in his dress. But now, he appeared to her to be too heavily cloaked – too heavily shaded – by the thick tweed jacket he was wearing; and his tie looked as if it had been tugged into position, not tied. Moreover, although his beard looked reasonably trim, she had noticed a curious thrust of hair that appeared to be sprouting from one side of his head, and that made him look unbalanced. And his eyes too looked strange. Not sad; but questioning and turned inwards.

What bothered her even more were the huge bruise and scar that still showed at one side of his forehead. 'Have you had some kind of accident?' she had asked. 'No,' he had replied, 'just a knock'; not nonchalantly exactly, but as if he didn't wish to say to her what the real cause of it had been. 'Oh,' Jason's mother had then answered, with a puzzled look in her eyes.

And as she said this, Jason had turned to look at her more directly, and to admire, as he had always done, the clean lines of her fine, near classical features; and knowing that he would always find her hair brushed neatly over her ears, and tied back in a loose bun; and that her skin would be as lightly tanned as it always was – even in winter; and that he would find her pale, grey eyes expressing patience and concern; but with no reflection in them of the turbulence that he was now experiencing in himself.

Could he speak to her, he wondered, about the change that was now taking place in his life?; and about the growing pressure he felt to abandon all self-discipline: to break free of the ties he had made over the years; of all the limits he had defined; and of all the restrictions that had checked him for so long? Could she – would she understand, that he had reached some kind of crisis-point of the mind? Or should he speak to his father about it? Would a few words with him offer the strength he felt so in need of? Their relationship had never been a really close one. The one he had had with his mother had been the dominant one of his life. She had been so much his guide, his mentor, his confidante, and had encouraged him to write as he grew older and then eventually to wed. And when he had been left such a generous sum of money by his grandfather, it was his mother's suggestion that he should retire from the teaching post he had held since leaving the army, in order to devote himself to writing. For she imagined that that is what she would have done herself, had she been in Jason's position. Not because she had ambitions in that direction – in the one of writing, that is – and that she was projecting onto Jason. For although she did like books and words, it was not in the way that Betty did; or that her husband did, for that matter; who seemed to be perpetually engrossed in literature of one kind or another; and most of which was concerned with scientific subjects, since that was the world that interested him the most.

Would his father be more objective, Jason wondered – more detached? Should he ask to see him alone, for once; in his study, perhaps, where he spent so much of his time? Or would his father simply reject him? – tell him to pull himself together?: unlikely though that seemed, since it was what his father was always being told to do himself, by the two women in the house. When he forgot things, for example (such as to button up his trousers), or when he seemed to be too lost in his thoughts, and not responding to questions that had been put to him. 'Oh, Edgar,' his wife would sometimes say to him with a light laugh, when she felt that he had abandoned her (perhaps regarding some domestic issue that had to be settled) 'I do wish that you would pull yourself together.'

Or should he say nothing to either of them? Could this be something that he was meant to keep to himself; and must not speak about, and must only write about in his notebooks? Was this, in other words, something that would be beyond his parents' understanding, and with which neither of them could cope? He certainly didn't see them as being the cause of his condition: didn't blame them, in the way that so many blame their parents for their troubles. At least he was wise enough to have realised that his troubles were his own – truly his own; and that nothing that had been done, or that had been said to him in childhood, could be named as being the root cause of his dilemma – which, as he now saw it (and as he was now able to see quite vividly) was the one of whether or not he might be capable of reconstructing his identity; or whether to do that, in view of the encounters it entailed – the *self*-encounters, that is – might be beyond him; and that what he might be forced to do, would be to accept the strictures of the life he had already formed. Accept his work, its method; accept the general shallow cleverness of his writing: accept his loneliness, his pain, his separation from his children and his wife — that he knew must soon lead to a divorce; and by some sheer effort of the will (for he knew that that is what it would require of him) attempt to maintain the mask that he had constructed for himself, and behind which he had always lived.

'You do know that they are coming here, don't you, Jason?' his mother had then asked, breaking the silence between them, that had been formed by Jason's ruminative thoughts. 'The children, I mean. And that Jill is coming with them?'

Jason looked at his mother as if he hadn't heard what she had said, and she felt embarrassed by it.

'Jill did tell you,' she added nervously, 'didn't she, Jason? . . . She is in touch with you.'

'Yes,' Jason replied. 'She did. She is.'

'Well,' his mother said, trying to assume an air of natural cheerfulness, 'it will be nice to see them again . . . Jill too . . . She tells me that she is looking forward to it.'

'And so she should be,' answered Jason, in the curiously pompous manner that he would adopt from time to time. 'Shouldn't she?' he then added, smiling, almost laughing to himself, as if the subject might be too much for him; and as he looked around him at the beauty of the garden, and at the dreamy, dark facade of the house; and then at Betty, who had just come out to join them, and who was carrying a newspaper in her hand.

'I thought you might like to see the paper,' she said to Jason, offering it to him. 'Not that there's much in it,' she remarked, as if for her there never was; and expressing the disdain she felt for the world of daily news and gossip; as opposed to the fictional one that she so enjoyed, and that so inspired her; and in which she always felt herself to be so naturally at home.

The next day, now back in London, Jason made this entry in his notebook:

'I was yesterday at my parents'. There for a two-day visit, and not having seen them for some time. I wish I could have stayed longer. The peace, the calm – the splendid order of the place: and my father hiding behind his spectacles and dear old Betty and her books. All so healing – so refreshing; were it not for the creeping fear I felt when there that the blood I fear to spill, and that the gods forbid I might yet *have* to spill, would so poison and pollute that lovely world. And it – what is happening to me – has nothing to do with them, with my parents. Of that I am certain. Perhaps my mother did project upon me too much when I was small; and certainly more than she did upon Jeremy; who always seemed to fight her and reject her. And perhaps, for a while, she did attempt to use me as some kind of object of her desire. But then, don't all mothers do that? If not with every child, then at least with one, or with some of their children? And don't all children know the power there can be in that? The power it gives *them*, I mean, over their parents; and which a great many of them use, as I did, artfully, and with skill: to further themselves; to gain advantages; prolong security: draw energy – knowing, if they are truly honest (and I have always done my best to be *that* in this matter) that later, as they grew up and out of childhood, they would need to break the ties that have been formed by that projection: and that to describe all this as being a *fault* of their parents is wrong. It is a fault if you like of them both – of both parent and child: a shared one: and one for which they must both be held responsible.

'Certainly, those are the feelings I have regarding my relationship with my mother. I *know* I am not the son that she believed me to be; and that I cannot – could never – be that. And I know too that I have done my best to tell her that this is so, and to help her see and accept it – as I think all children have a need to do, gradually, over the years. But what I *do* feel concerned about is the fault, or flaw, that there seems to be in myself. Not a fault or flaw of a moral kind. No one could have done more than I have done to live a decent life: to do all the 'right', all the accepted things: to have been a good soldier during the war: a good father to my children; a good husband to my wife. No, the fault I speak about, and that I feel a need to write about is similar to ones in geological affairs: the fault of an earth structure, for example – or of a rock structure, rather – which means that there is an inherent weakness in it: one not showing, but lying beneath the surface, and by means of which volcanic eruptions can occur.

'This is what I should have faced in myself a long time ago, but have avoided all my life: that I am an imperfect being: that I am a marred or damaged one; and that there are within me, hidden desires, hidden drives that – oh, I don't know *how* to speak of them! Not yet. I cannot say; cannot yet write of them, however much I may want to; may feel a need to do. Perhaps later I will. Perhaps in a while I shall be able to. For the moment, I am too tired – too exhausted by these encounters, and can say, can write, no more.

'I do not believe in a God; or not in any God that is personified by religion. Not in a Heavenly Father, I mean, or a Holy Ghost, or a Heavenly Son (yet please take note of my use of capital letters, which just shows how I was brought up!). No, the only God I know of seems a stumbling, clumsy, imperfect thing; incapable, it would appear, of getting things right: full of mistakes, accidents, errors; making so much of what he, or she, had created dependent upon mere chance.

'So if I choose to rail against all *that*, am I wrong? Is the anger I feel irreligious? Somehow, I do not think so.'

During the next few days, Jason felt a little relieved of the pressures that had been bothering him – or that had been threatening him, rather, for such was the intensity of the emotion they could arouse; and he half believed that the various notes he had been setting down, and in which he had voiced a few of his troubles, had in some way cured him. For he now no longer gave in to them when he found himself not wanting to answer his telephone. And if he found himself wandering the streets at all, without knowing exactly why, it would never last for very long, and it certainly happened a lot less often than it had done.

However, if Jason's life was calmer and quieter for a while, and if he gained some much needed relief from that, it was a relief that proved to be only a temporary one, alas. For within days the tensions in him returned, that made him feel so unwell and insecure; and he was again forced to confront the mirror and the monster that he had seen there and had recognised; and which, if he was to be truthful, he knew had been there always; had always lurked beneath the surface of his orderly, daytime world.

Was he more ape than man? Jason asked himself, as his dark, questioning eyes found their counterpoints in the mirror. Had the hair on his chest and shoulders grown thicker in recent years? Was the new heaviness of his flesh, that made him want to be wrapped in coats and scarves when he went out, in what was still quite warm, late-summer weather, an expression of that blocked, closed area of his mind that could still not face the truth of what he was; or of what he might be; and that he had somehow managed, over the years, to resist confronting?

'I think I'll give myself a drink,' Jason would often tell himself, in such moments of self-confrontation; 'and then go out to have something to eat, perhaps' – thinking where he might go to spoil himself; to find some particular dish that might be a favourite of his; or where he knew the wine would be good, or the waiters and waitresses polite; and summoning up all the defences he could muster to protect himself; sometimes muttering to himself (as he was changing to go out, perhaps) that he really *ought* to speak to his wife, or to Tom and Sarah, his children; both of which were things that he seldom actually did, since he usually left it to his wife to take the initiative in the exchanges they were still having; and then leaving his rooms in a hurried, furtive manner; not bothering to look around him as he left, in order to be sure that the windows were closed, or that all the taps had been turned off; and pulling his door to behind him with a slam – so that Arnold, whose ears were attuned to all the noises of the house, would say to Lottie, if she was with him, 'There he goes, Lottie – our mystery man. I wonder who he's got going out with him tonight? . . . Well, it's not going to be me, darling – is it? *That's* for sure. In fact, I can't think when it was that *I* last went out with a man. Not that I feel at all sorry for myself, you know; not when I've got friends like you, dear; and like John and Billy. And we do have our fun at times, don't we, Lottie dear? Our little chats; our little gossips. We do still have our moments, Lottie – don't we?'

And in response to which, one can imagine how Lottie might answer him with one of her hard, lustrous smiles:

then say, 'But I still don't like the look of that man, you know.'

'Oh! *Don't* you?' one can hear Arnold reply.

'No, Arnold, I don't. He's not my type. I dislike men who are secretive. I don't care for the dark, brooding kind: the Mr Rochesters of this world. I never have.'

'Oh *dear*, Lottie,' Arnold might then have answered with a chuckle, 'what *do* you like, I wonder? Do we have to find you a Nordic airline pilot, or something? Someone blond, clean-limbed, clean-shaven?

'Could be,' Lottie might then have said to him in return, and speaking ambiguously; because she had chosen to guard, even from him, a secret she kept strictly to herself; which was that as far as that sort of thing was concerned – meaning, her taste in sexual partners – what she really liked was not men, but going to bed with women.

PART THREE

X

THERE CAN BE little that is light or humorous in the next
few pages of this novel, since there can be nothing in them
of Arnold and his world, or of the world of Betty and her
books. For we must now move north to Cumbria and its
Lake District, and to the house of Jason's mother-in-law;
a tall, stern, dry-skinned widow, who was now in her
mid-sixties, and who lived with her daughter, Gillian (or
Jill, as she was more often called, and by almost everyone
but her mother); as well as with Tom and Sarah, her
two grandchildren, who had been out all day on their
bicycles, and who, having so tired themselves, and having
hurriedly eaten their supper, had suddenly taken themselves
off to bed.

'There, Mother. Peace and quiet for once,' said Gillian
with a smile, looking up from a crossword-puzzle she had
been studying.

'Yes. They do stay up rather late,' answered her mother,
not smiling in return, and stifling any twinge of conscience
she might have regarding her daughter's need of affection.
'I wish they would tire themselves more often.'

'I know. But they *are* in their teens, Mother,' Gillian
answered defensively.

'Yes. I am aware of that,' said her mother, tugging at one
of her earlobes, which was a habit of hers; then fingering
the string of cut-glass beads she was wearing, the hard glitter

of which found a reflection in her eyes. 'Nonetheless, they are still children, Gillian. You are forgetting that, I think.'

'Not when they are in need of something!' Gillian answered, now with a laugh, and still in the hope that she might provoke at least a smile from her mother in return.

'Yes. Well. You do spoil them, I am afraid.'

'Do I, Mother?'

'Yes. You do. When *we* were small; when your father and I were small; we didn't have half the things that children have today.'

'But the world changes, Mother.'

'Oh, it certainly does. And it is made obvious, Gillian, if I can say so, by your going through with this divorce . . . I know you don't like me to speak about it, but you do realise that I dislike what you have done; or what you are about to do, rather . . . I mean, why *did* you leave your husband? You haven't explained it. Not to me. Nor to anyone, it seems. It isn't as if Jason was a drunk or something – was he? – As your father was. I mean to say, *I* would have had grounds for such an action. Not because your father was physically violent. He was never that. But he certainly was a drunk – or a drunk of sorts, at least; as a lot of men were in those days. And women too, for that matter; although *their* drinking was usually done in secret, of course.'

Gillian bit her lip, then suddenly blurted out, 'I'm sorry, Mother. It isn't that I don't *want* to talk about it, it is simply that I can't.'

'But why ever *not*?' her mother persisted, in spite of having brought tears to her daughter's eyes. 'Is it something so awful? So unspeakable? Did Jason hurt you physically – damage you? Or was it something to do with the children? . . . He didn't harm *them*, I hope.'

'No, Mother!' protested Gillian. 'There was nothing

like *that*. It is just that — well, that Jason and I have differences.'

'Differences? You mean of taste, Gillian? Of opinion? You mean, you left your husband, Gillian; you mean you walked out on him, and came up here with the children, on account of *that* — of differences? . . . Well . . . That hardly makes sense, does it? And on what grounds, I might ask, can you seek a divorce if that is the cause you have to give? Violence, yes — although not always, you know; since a wife's assertions aren't always believed. Or adultery. Yes that too. But certainly not because of differences . . . Are you simply saying that the two of you just bickered?'

Gillian rose from her chair and crossed to a window. 'The room is cold,' she said, as she stretched to pull the window shut; and then to secure it.

'Yes. It is,' said her mother with a shiver, drawing a light shawl around her shoulders: 'and it can be here, you know, once September has set in. Hot during the day, but cold and misty at night.'

'Well, there is no mist at least,' said Gillian, glad to have diverted the conversation, and as she looked up at the dark night sky, and at the dense cluster of trees that had been planted far too close to the house; which gave its downstairs rooms an almost perpetual air of gloom; and masked any daytime view they would otherwise have of the lake.

'But with all of us gone, you are going to have plenty of peace tomorrow,' said Gillian, as she went back to her chair.

'Yes — and that's another thing: your going to the Callows. That seems strange as well. I can understand that the children should go. The Callows are their grandparents. But surely, there's no need for you to go too. Isn't it rather odd for you to be doing that?'

'They are nice people, Mother. I am fond of them. I

always have been. Mr Callow especially. I don't see why I shouldn't be friendly with them.'

'Perhaps you should ask your husband that question, Gillian.'

'Ask Jason? Oh, but he would approve. I *know* he would. I know he *does*, in fact. Jason doesn't blame me, Mother, for what has happened; any more than I blame him. We are both confused, perhaps; but we both know that we weren't meant to stay together: that we couldn't; and — well — we are both trying to be civilised about it.'

'Oh, civilised! That's an expression everyone uses today. We saw in the war what being civilised means — didn't we? Making a mess of things, it seems to me.'

Gillian heard the bitterness in her mother's voice. It was a bitterness she had always known — had always recognised, even when a child; and she had always recoiled from it, believing it to be venomous in some way, and that it was something from which she should protect herself. So she collected her mother's coffee cup and saucer and quickly left the room; calling out as she went, 'I hope those two haven't left some awful mess in the kitchen.'

'Oh, they will have,' her mother muttered to herself, her eyes searching restlessly for something upon which to settle: her birdlike head making quick, darting movements as she eagerly scanned the room.

'Gillian!' she then called out — loudly.

'Yes, Mother?' Gillian answered from the kitchen.

'Those oat biscuits of mine . . . The ones I have for breakfast . . . You will make sure that there are some on my breakfast-tray — won't you?'

'I have already done that, Mother.'

'Oh — have you?'

'Yes, Mother: your pills as well.'

'Oh, my pills. Yes,' said her mother, as her eyes finally came to rest upon a framed photograph of herself on her wedding-day, in which she was dressed in a particularly well-cut moiré suit, the look of which still pleased her; reminding her, as it did, of the good taste that she had always had in clothes.

When he next paid Jason a visit, which was for the first time after the 'accident', as the two friends had come to name it, Joseph Mallory, Jason's painter-friend, was still possessed by ideas concerning the theatre: which had now shifted away from Bertolt Brecht, and the announced arrival of his theatre company in London, and had directed themselves towards Shakespeare; and towards one play of his in particular. For he had been to see a production at The Old Vic of Shakespeare's *Coriolanus*, in which Richard Burton had played the lead, and had given a performance that had impressed him.

'Bloody good actor that,' he had said to Jason, soon after he had arrived; 'and a rattling good story too . . . Do you know it, Jason?'

'I *think* I do,' Jason answered. 'Coriolanus is a soldier. A general.'

'Yes; and a bloody good one. The Romans worshipped him: thought him a god; or something close to one.'

'But he gets killed, does he? Murdered?'

'At the end, yes. But, you know, I was thinking, Jason, what a mistake that is – on Shakespeare's part . . . I mean, I think he got it wrong, you know. Bloody marvellous play until then, but –'

'But what?'

'But – well, he shouldn't have had Coriolanus killed; murdered; by the Volscians.'

'Who were what? Rome's enemy?'

'Yes . . . Coriolanus is a soldier, as you said; and a great one; but he's got this bee in his fucking bonnet about wanting to become something more. He wants to become a consul – or his mother wants him to, at least: a member of the Senate; the equivalent of becoming a Member of Parliament, I suppose. *But*, to do that he's got to humble himself – hasn't he? In front of the Roman crowd; in public; because – well – because that was the Roman custom. And he can't fucking well *do* it – can he? Because – well, because he's too bloody *proud* to do it – that's why.'

'And so?' asked Jason, only half recalling the story.

'So he gets the crowd's back up – doesn't he? Makes them bloody furious.'

'Yes – that's right. I remember,' said Jason, wondering exactly where Joseph's thoughts might be leading him.

'Well, then, you'll remember too I expect that the people, the Roman workers, if you like, get so fucking annoyed with him; so incensed by him; they say they're going to throw him off a bloody rock.'

'But they don't.'

'That's right. Coriolanus's upper-class friends manage to rescue him: manage to get him away – out of Rome altogether; leaving his family behind him: his wife, his mother, and his little boy.'

'And then what?'

'Well – what does he bloody well go and do but make up to the Volscians! *That's* what! Walks straight up to their leader – an old toughie, called Aufidius – and offers to join him. Offers to join Rome's *enemy*, that is! In order, I suppose, to get his revenge: upon Rome; for kicking him out.'

'And then?' asked Jason, still not sure where Joseph's ideas were taking him.

'Well, he does do it. He *does* join the Volscian army; and there's this bloody great speech – homo-erotic, I suppose you could call it – in which Aufidius says something to Coriolanus about their having gone down together in their sleep, and words like that; expressing a form of bonding, I presume: the result being that the two of them – Coriolanus and Aufidius together – then march against Rome: both of them leading the Volscian army.'

'And they conquer it? Is that what happens?'

'Yes. But there's no fight: no battle – *that's* the bloody point. The Romans are so shit scared, so bloody frightened, they just give in, just fucking well surrender. And there's this famous scene, you see, when they send Coriolanus's mother out of the city to beg her son for mercy: on Rome's behalf, as it were; so she's obviously some kind of figurehead. And she brings with her his wife and his son – his little boy – as a form of emotional back-up, if you like: to make a big scene of it, you might say. So what you get is wife, mother and child begging the son, the father and the husband not to attack.'

'And he does? Or he doesn't?'

'No, of *course* he fucking well doesn't. He's a *soldier*, Jason; and won't fight when there's no need to fight. No soldier's going to do *that* . . . I mean, he's got his revenge – hasn't he – without a single sword being drawn? Got the Romans on their bloody knees, he has. Shit scared of him. *And* of Aufidius too; *and* of the Volscian army.'

'And?'

'Well. He could have had anything he bloody well wanted – couldn't he? Could have gone back to Rome; could have become a consul even; a member of the Senate: could have had anything he fucking well wanted out of them.'

'But what? He didn't.'

'No.'

'And?'

'Well, that's the point I'm *getting* at, Jason,' said Joseph, showing some irritation. 'Why *didn't* he? What made him *not* do that, is what I want to know. I mean, there was his mother: there was his wife, his child – right there in front of him – all crying their fucking eyes out; and what does he do? Nothing. Just agrees not to sack Rome – that's all. Achieves a conquest, just like that; but takes no personal advantage of it *what*soever. Now, *that's* bloody weird, it seems to me. Fucking spooky.'

'And so?' asked Jason, the story now finding strange echoes in his mind, and asking the question more of himself than of his friend.

'So Shakespeare just has him killed – that's what; by the Volscians; by Rome's enemy: which is sheer bloody nonsense. I mean, *why*? Why kill someone who's just led them to such a triumph: to such a victory. Of course, it makes for a bloody good scene. A vicious killing, with trumpets and drums after it, like at the end of *Hamlet*; to round the play off. But to my mind it just doesn't make sense . . . And I'll tell you something else, Jason.'

'Like what?'

'Like it looks as if old Shakespeare hadn't done his bloody homework.'

'Homework?' said Jason, with a sudden laugh; enjoying Joseph's twists and turns of thought.

'Yes. He'd read Plutarch: obviously; because that's how the story ends in Plutarch's version of it. But what he *hadn't* done was to read Livy; because do you know what? Livy says – *he* says – that according to the earliest Roman authority – Fabius, I think he's called – Coriolanus *didn't* die. He *wasn't* murdered, he says; neither by the Volscian soldiers, nor by their leader, Aufidius. All that happened was that he simply didn't go back to Rome. Didn't go back to his wife, his mother or his son. Instead, he remained *with* the Volscians, in exile, as it were; and became I guess, a kind of recluse – or that's what Livy seems to indicate. As if, once he'd got what he *thought* he wanted, which was revenge, he then realised that it wasn't what he fucking well wanted at all! And that he'd been given a chance for once to find out who he *really* was; which was *not* to be a servant of the bloody State: *not* to be a soldier; not even a consul, nor even a husband or a father: but to be simply alone, facing himself . . . Now, that's a really *modern* story, it seems to me, Jason. And I don't think old Shakespeare was quite up to it, do you? Or at least, that's how I'm seeing it at the moment, Jason. Those are my thoughts: my ideas.'

Jason didn't know how he might answer that question. All he knew was that he had suddenly found something of himself in Joseph's version of that story. That he too had turned his back upon the 'done' – the 'accepted' things. Why, he still didn't know. What was driving him into *his* form of exile was still beyond him. But Joseph's talk had helped to ease his mind. It had been a piece of cheek, he thought, for Joseph to have said what he had about Shakespeare; that he hadn't been 'quite up to it'; but as was so often the case with his friend, his soaring, free-wheeling thoughts had been a refreshment to his mind, and he felt sorry when Joseph left; which was in a somewhat abrupt manner; mostly because the two of them would always avoid any really personal exchange of emotion. Even their farewell handshake had been only a light one – no more than a tip of the cap; after which, Joseph had merely patted Jason lightly upon the shoulder, saying that it was time he was out and about; and protesting at his having to still visit him in his rooms, rather than meet him out in a local bar; which he would have enjoyed doing more, because they would then not be alone; and because – although he was far from being at all conscious of this – there would be plenty of other men around them.

For several days, Jason hadn't left his rooms, and had been neglecting himself, as far as food was concerned; living mainly on cans of food and bread that he would buy from a small grocery shop nearby. And it was now some time since he had seen his new 'friends', as he had come to call them, John and Billy; mostly because he had come to think that he had been using them far too much, and which had made him feel guilty and self-conscious. He had thanked them profusely for their kindnesses, when he had told them that he could now manage on his own; and they had insisted in return that if he did happen to need them, then he must get in touch with them at once – which he hadn't yet done, but which he had certainly thought of doing on several occasions; not because of any need he had, but because he so missed their cheer and their company.

That evening, after Joseph had left, and after he had written yet another entry in his new notebook, which he had placed under the heading, 'Some thoughts about Coriolanus', and in which he had made a kind of précis of Joseph's ideas (and which he had felt a need to set down so that he could return to them from time to time), he decided that he would risk going out to a restaurant for a meal; quite a smallish one, and not too far from where he lived; and one in which he was always treated with respect, in the sense that the staff would only speak to him if he spoke to them; and would never ask questions of him of a prying kind.

Before changing, however, he found himself thinking of John and Billy; wondering how they were and what they might be doing; and he felt a really strong temptation to ring them up; not knowing that they, at the same time, were having the same thoughts about him.

'John . . . I wonder how he is – how Mr Callow is?' said Billy, as he stepped out of the shower, and as he began to rub himself vigorously with a towel; watched closely by his friend, who always found the sight of Billy's naked body so alluring, and full of a bright, quick energy that he lacked.

'Funny you should say that,' answered John. 'I was just thinking that myself.'

'Were you really?' said Billy.

'Yes,' said John. 'I was wondering if we should give him a buzz, perhaps; just to see that he is all right.'

'Do you think we could?' asked Billy.

'Well, I don't see why not,' answered John, as he watched Billy fuss over the drying of his groin. 'I don't know about *me*, but I'm sure he'd be pleased to hear from *you*.'

'Oh, rubbish,' said Billy. 'Don't start that again – making out Mr Callow's got a crush on me. Because he hasn't.'

'I don't think he's got a crush on anyone,' said John, more seriously. 'Do you?'

'Perhaps not,' said Billy. 'I've never thought about it.'

'Well, shall we, or shan't we?'

'What? Ring him?'

'Yes,' said John.

'Oh – well – I don't know. Later perhaps. What do you think?'

'Well, later then; if we do. Yes.'

'Yes,' said Billy, knowing as he did so that they probably wouldn't ring Jason at all; not because they weren't fond of him, for they had both become that during the short time that they had looked after him; but because they had been so intimidated by the number of books he had in his rooms; and by the number of letters there were as well, that were stacked here and there; and a number of which seemed to be spilling from a large wooden bowl, that was kept on the sturdy, gatelegged table that Jason occasionally used as a desk; and by the knowledge too that Jason was an author, and quite a well-known author at that – which, combined with the considerable differences between them in age (they had calculated that there must be almost a quarter of a century between them), created a kind of barrier in their minds, that they felt too shy to overcome.

'Or he'll ring us, perhaps,' Billy added, once he had finished drying himself, and had put on a clean pair of underpants, and was disporting himself before John; half curled up in a chair: and as if he might be some kind of angel – or some kind of cherub perhaps, would be better words for describing him.

XI

JASON CAME HOME late that night, feeling disturbed again and upset. He had eaten too much, drunk too much, and seemed to have returned to his old, bad habits. Moreover, he had experienced something on the way home that had affected him so very deeply that he believed it to be something he must face, and that he would need to write about in his notebook.

There had been rain during the early part of the evening, so the streets were damp and cool, and there were no people about – or very few, at least; which was often the case in Chelsea in those days. Then, as he left the King's Road, and as he turned into one of the side-streets that lead to the river, he found himself being attracted by a sudden glitter of light, that was reflecting from a pavement-edge ahead of him, quite close to a pedestrian crossing.

'At first, I wondered what this odd glitter of light could be,' Jason later wrote in his notebook. 'Then, as I drew closer, I could see that the source of it was a scattering of small fragments of glass, that were strewn across the pavement's edge, and that then spilled into the road. And I knew at once – simply because I have seen such a thing before, and have seen it many times, in fact – that they must be the splintered and scattered fragments of a car's headlamps; or of its windscreen, perhaps; and guessed immediately that it meant there had been an accident. What so disturbed me, however, and is why I feel that I must write about it now; so soon after it occurred; so that it cannot dissolve into daily time, where so many things are disposed of and forgotten; is that no sooner had my eye assessed what the cause of this glitter of light must be, than I noticed at its centre (as if it might be at the heart or centre of a wound) a dark red stain or mark, the greater part of which was on the pavement, as opposed to on the road.

'Was this the mark of blood? was the first thought that came into my head. Had someone been injured, or even died, perhaps – here, just a short time ago? Was this, I asked myself, the blood of some other human being than myself, that I didn't know, and that I had not set eyes on in my life, that was marking the pavement of this quiet, Chelsea thoroughfare . . . ? And no sooner did I think those thoughts than I noticed that my heart had begun to beat rapidly, and my brain to race and pulse with some feverish kind of excitement. Why? I kept asking. One could say, perhaps, that this might have been the reaction of anyone; and that without their being particularly conscious of it, this combination of bloodstains and splintered glass would be bound to affect them in this manner. Yet I know that the excitement I felt was not of a kind that most people would experience. Moreover, my body-temperature soared, and for a moment I felt uncomfortably hot – which is a rare thing for me these days, as I am usually feeling quite the reverse of that, and find that I need to wear extra or unseasonable clothing, such as the thick tweed coat I wore when I last visited my parents; or the old striped scarf, that I now keep wrapped around my neck, and that I seem to wear at almost any time of the day or night – which I am aware must give me something of an eccentric appearance; as if I am beginning to find some kind of tramp in me, that wants to retreat from public life, and to be imprisoned within the smaller world of his own few personal possessions.

'Then, as I drew close to the pedestrian crossing, where the street lighting was a little stronger, and which had provided the source of light that was being reflected from the pavement and the road, I came to the edge of what one might call this spill of shattered glass – and found, to my astonishment, that instead of stepping around it in order to pass, and in order to continue on my way home, I deliberately stepped *into* it! Some form of cunning in me made me first check to see that I was alone in the street, and that no one was peering at me from some nearby window; and then (I can recall how I almost trembled as I did this) I crouched down, there on that pavement's edge, and rubbed my fingertips against the dark stain of what I already felt so sure must be the dark stain of blood.

'And as I touched it, half expecting – indeed, half hoping, I have to confess – that it would still be wet, or would be a little moist, at least, I felt as if some electric charge, or current, had been forced into me; and without hesitation, I spread my palm wide and pressed my entire hand upon the ground, partly grazing myself with some of the sharp chippings of glass, but not caring, even if I had been injured more seriously: even if they had inflicted upon me some more substantial wound; and if I had returned home with a bleeding, lacerated hand.

'Fortunately, the latter didn't occur, and here I am, after having washed and disinfected the few nicks and grazes I suffered, and wondering what all this has been about.

'I said, when I began this series of notes, that I would do my best to tell the truth in them about myself – warts and wrinkles and all; but it now looks as if it might be something more than a detailed, Flemish portrait I have to paint; as if it is not the outer things I am seeing, with all the defects and imperfections that any flesh is naturally heir to, but some more reluctant – some more lurking kind of figure, that is unaccustomed to the light. Some thing of darkness it would seem that I must acknowledge; and, whether I care to do so or not, that I must recognise as mine!'

The following morning, Jason received a phone call from his publisher, who said to him, with a hint of annoyance in his voice, that he had rung him several times during the past few weeks, and was wanting to know why he'd not heard from him, or had not seen him for some time. Was he working? he wanted to know. Was there another of his books in the 'pipeline', perhaps? One that he could count upon, that is; as well as other various questions of the kind that publishers ask. And reflecting the fact that Jason was a reasonably established figure in the literary world, who was now expected to produce his particular kind of book at regular, well-paced intervals.

Jason had been delighted by the way in which he had dealt with all this; by saying that yes, he was certainly writing, but not very regularly; and that whether or not it would turn itself into a book he had no idea: which in turn had provoked a further round of questions from his publisher, attempting to coax Jason into revealing exactly what *kind* of piece of writing it was that he had been speaking about.

'Sounds interesting,' his publisher had then answered,

with a nervous tremble in his voice, after evidently having been baffled by Jason's replies. 'Oh, does it?' Jason then asked, with a light laugh: to which he had added, in order to end the conversation, 'Well, Roger, all I know is that I am saying things that I have never dared to say in my life. Things which, to be frank with you, I doubt that my readers will enjoy.'

'Oh,' had been his publisher's answer to that. 'Well, we'll have to see, Jason – won't we?': then, with a nervous, high-pitched giggle he had hurriedly put the phone down, and so brought their talk to an end.

'Lottie. You know that woman – the one who lives across the street from me?'

'What woman, Arnold?'

'Oh, you know. The one who wears those enormous strings of pearls and a floppy, velvet blue hat. Lady something or another she is; or she says she is, at least.'

'No,' said Lottie, with no expression whatsoever, 'I've never heard of her – or seen her, for that matter.'

'But Lottie, you *have*. I *know* you have.'

'Well, what about her?'

'What about her? Well, it seems she's nothing more than a tart.'

'A *what*?' said Lottie.

'A tart – a prostitute. Men going in and out of the place all day. Bertie Wooster types, most of them. You know; pink faces – blond, usually; and looking too frightened to wipe their own bottoms.'

'Arnold! What a thing to say!'

'Well – you know what I *mean*, don't you, dear? Public school types: puritanical; and looking for a good whipping. Wanting matron to put them across her knee.'

'Where on earth do you get those ideas from, Arnold? Who's been telling you this? Is it John and Billy?'

'No. It's got nothing to do with them. I've just been keeping a sharp look-out, Lottie – that's all. Nothing better to do, you see. After all, I've got to pass my days doing *some*thing – haven't I? Unless *you* come round. And especially now, when I'm no longer able to read.'

'Well, I've told you about that,' said Lottie. 'We're going to see an optician.'

'Oh, yes, dear; I know we are. Very sweet of you. But I don't think they'll be able to do much for me, you know. I'm going blind, Lottie, and that's all there is to it.'

'Arnold!' exclaimed Lottie, alarmed by Arnold's comment regarding the declining state of his health.

'Well, it's the truth. And it's always better to face it. That's been my motto all my life. But I'm not so blind as yet not to be able to see that that Lady Letitia, or whatever she calls herself, is running some kind of posh, upper-class brothel. Not that it's really news to me. I've always suspected her of it. For one thing, her make-up gives her away. Enough powder on her face to flour a damned pastry-board, I should think.'

'I don't know that a person's make-up is a sign of anything,' said Lottie, reflecting upon what people might think of Arnold.

'Oh, *I* think it is, Lottie. A true lady doesn't plaster it on like that – and *I* should know. Just a light dusting, dear, is all that it needs; to mask the pimples and the sores.'

'Well, what if she does?' said Lottie. 'What if she does run a brothel? What difference does it make? It's not as if she's someone you actually *know*, Arnold; so why be bothered by it?'

'Oh, I'm not bothered by it, dear. I quite like it, in fact. To tell you the truth, she's rather colourful, I find; and far more interesting than those fussy old dears you see around Sloane Square. The ones with their little black, patent court shoes; and their crimpled hair and dresses. No, I like her.

She's got a touch of Nell Gwyn about her, it seems to me. Not that she doles out oranges, as far as I know: though she doles out lots of other things, I expect.'

'And what about your neighbour?' Lottie then asked, pausing in the act of arranging the curls of her snow-white fringe; that were always made to show a little beneath the brims of her pudding-shaped hats.

'My neighbour? Who do you mean?'

'The one upstairs. The writer. What news is there of him? Do John and Billy still see him?'

'John and Billy? No. I don't think so. No, they don't go there now – not any longer. Not since he's been better.'

'Oh. So he's better then?'

'Yes. Or at least I think he is – although I've not seen him for several days; and even when I did last see him, I didn't actually speak to him. I just saw him from the landing, as he was about to leave the house. Still, he looked all right; more or less; wearing some kind of funny old scarf around his neck, and looking a little scruffy, I thought; but he's well, I think; or well enough, considering how he was; though to be frank with you, Lottie, I've not given much thought to him of late. We've never been close, you know. Just good neighbours. He's not really my type. Too much of an intellectual one for me.'

Lottie smiled at this, her taut eyelids quickly pleating themselves as she looked across the room at Arnold, and as they revealed the striking beauty of her purple-violet-blue eyes, which she knew to be the most salient of her features, and that she also knew how to use to some effect.

Arnold died the following day – or rather during the night-time hours that concluded it; and was found, as he had always said would be the case, in the early part of the next morning. Not by Jason, but by John and Billy, who had been told by Lottie the night before that Arnold wasn't too well; and after ringing him several times since breakfast but without receiving a reply, had assumed that something must be wrong.

'Stay here,' John said to Billy, as he crossed the hallway of Arnold's apartment.

'Why?' asked Billy, ignoring John's command: then turning white as he followed John into the living-room and saw the half-naked body of Arnold sprawled out upon the carpet; with his hairpiece free of his head, and lying forlorn and mask-like beside him; and a thick, dried-up trickle of blood that streaked one side of his face.

'John. Is he dead?' asked Billy in a whisper.

John nodded. 'I think so.'

'What do we do?' asked Billy, nervously.

'We call a doctor,' John said authoritatively. 'And you run upstairs; and tell Mr Callow.'

'No, John! I don't think I can,' said Billy, as tears formed in his eyes.

'Of *course* you can,' said John, knowing that action would be the best thing for his friend. 'Go and tell him, now. Go *on*.'

Which Billy did; knocking gently on Jason's door and wondering for a moment if he was in.

'Good gracious,' said Jason, when he came to the door. 'Billy! Come in. What *is* it?'

'Arnold is dead,' said Billy, the tears now flowing freely down his cheeks.

Jason was silent for a moment. 'Is John there?' he then asked.

'Yes. He's calling a doctor.'

'Good,' said Jason, worrying that Billy was about to faint, or be sick or something. 'Here,' he said, 'sip this,' as he poured out a small nip of brandy and handed Billy the glass.

'What is it?' asked Billy.

'Brandy,' said Jason.

'I never touch it,' said Billy, defiantly. 'Nor whisky either.'

'It's medicine,' said Jason insistently, and feeling relieved when Billy obediently took a sip of it.

'Now – are you feeling better?' Jason then asked, after he had guided Billy to a chair. 'You were as white as a ghost a few minutes ago' – to which Billy only nodded in return.

'Now then. Shall we go down?' Jason said, 'or would you prefer to stay up here, perhaps?'

'No,' answered Billy, not liking to be made to feel that he was a weakling. 'I'll go down. I'll come with you.'

'Good,' said Jason, as he slipped off his dressing gown and as he stepped into a pair of trousers; feeling self-conscious in front of Billy, on account of the ungainly folds of flesh around his middle.

*

'Mummy. Is Grandad very old?' Jason's son, Tom, asked his mother.

'Well, he's quite old,' said Jill, who was sitting beside him in the train on the way to Hampshire.

'Yes, but I mean *very* old – like nearly a hundred or something.'

'Oh, no – of *course* not!' said Jill with a laugh. 'Why do you ask, Tom? Why do you want to know?'

'Because Sarah says that he is – that's why. Don't you, Sarah?'

'I said just old, Tom: not a hundred.'

'Well, to be honest,' said their mother, 'I don't know what age he is exactly. But older than your grandmother is, in any case.'

'Than Grandma Callow, you mean,' said Tom.

'Yes, of course. Quite a lot older, I think.'

'I like him,' said Sarah, straightening her dress.

'And so do I,' said Jill, who was looking forward to seeing her in-laws again.

'I prefer Grandma,' said Tom, as the train came to a halt, and as they arrived at their destination.

'And Mummy; is Daddy going to be there?' Sarah then asked, as they approached the ticket-barrier, and as her mother handed in the tickets.

'No. I don't think so,' Jill answered firmly; but still harbouring a vague hope that they might find him waiting to greet them when they arrived; and seeing Jason in her mind as he had been when they were young, with his curly, auburnish hair tumbling over his ears, and when his smile had at times been almost radiant; and when, as she now suddenly remembered him, he had sometimes been a little clownish in his behaviour.

'No, Sarah,' Jill then repeated, 'he won't, I'm afraid,' as she and her children climbed into the hired car that had been sent to collect them.

'Oh,' said Sarah, with a pout, looking at Tom; who knew exactly what his sister was thinking; but who merely blinked his eyes at her in return.

And as they sped through the leafy lanes and byroads of Hampshire, and as the rays of the late afternoon sun cut low across the fields; piercing the passing trees and hedgerows, and casting a series of constantly changing shadows against the windows of the car; the family fell into silence. As if, all at once, they were sharing the same, collective thoughts; thoughts that were too deep perhaps for them to voice, and to have brought out into the open; but ones that needed some time of them; as well as a degree of their attention.

'Well,' said Jill eventually, 'here we are, I think,' as the car turned off the road and into a driveway and she saw Betty ahead of her, waving; and beyond her, on the steps of the house, her mother-in-law, who had come out to greet them as well, and who was obviously calling to her husband to suggest that he should do the same thing; and as the children suddenly became a little shy and formal, not quite liking to wave vigorously in return, in the way they remembered having done so very often when they were small, and that was now accompanied by slight pangs of regret.

'Well, Jill,' said Lilian Callow, once they had all settled in, and after Tom and Sarah had gone off with their grandfather for an evening stroll by the river, 'it really is good to have you here again. And the children too, of course. I was half frightened, you know, that we'd become cut off from each other; and I am so glad – so grateful – that we haven't . . . You still speak to Jason, I gather,' she then added, 'and that's another thing that I am pleased about.'

'Well, there are the children,' said Jill, 'so I have to. Not that Jason rings *me* very much. I'm afraid that I'm the one who usually takes the initiative.'

'Oh, I'm sorry,' said Lilian.

'Yes, so am I,' answered Jill. 'But there –'

'But there, what?'

'But there it is,' said Jill, first with a sigh and then a smile, and feeling a sudden sense of relief through having been able to express herself in this way. 'It has to be. I know it now. I seem to have accepted it at last. There are some things that cannot be changed, it seems; that cannot be different from how they are. I don't think, if I am to be honest, that Jason was ever meant to marry . . . And perhaps I wasn't either,' she then said, out of a wisdom that had formed in her of late, and because she was aware of what dangers there can be in projecting all one's troubles onto others: a perspective she had acquired since she had gone to live with her mother; and who, to her relief, she had at last ceased to think of as being the source of all that might be unloving in the world.

XII

ON THE DAY of Arnold's funeral, Jason wrote the following entry in his notebook:

'Today, my landlord, Arnold, is to be buried. Not burned, John told me was the expression Arnold had used. "When I go," he said, "I want to be buried, not burned. I don't want to give the Devil ideas."

'I like John. In many ways, he seems so much more of a man than I am. More in control of himself and of his life. Arnold's friend, Lottie, sent up a note, telling me that she was in charge of things — meaning of the funeral, I presumed, and that if I would care to go to it, she was sure that Arnold would be pleased. I've sent back a message, saying that I was sorry, but that I didn't feel quite up to it, having been ill and so forth; and addressed it just to 'Lottie', since she'd omitted to give me her surname; and have just slipped it beneath the door of Arnold's flat.

'Apart from the fact that I knew Arnold only a little, one reason for my not wanting to go to the funeral is the business of what to wear. Or, rather not *what* to wear exactly, because the answer to that is an obvious one; but because I would have to change into other clothes than the ones I am wearing at the moment

– and have been wearing *every* day: now, for over a week!

'Does this worry me? – bother me? This growing tramp-like thing I have of becoming attached to just one particular set of clothes; and wanting to virtually live in them? The answer is, when I think of it, yes; and no when I don't. Yet I would have quite liked to have been at Arnold's funeral; partly because of John and Billy; because to me, in my mind, they have become friends, and because I don't have too many of those these days, having pushed so many away. And as I have just said, I like John. In fact, I admire him. He's so different from the initial impression I had of him, when I first saw him with Billy on the stairs. As for Billy, he's more elusive; and if I am to be honest about it, I am not always sure how I should handle the feelings I have about him.

'Today is also the day that my wife and my two children are leaving my parents' house in Hampshire, and are returning to Cumbria after their brief holiday: and before the children return to school – or before Tom does, rather, and Sarah goes back to college. I had meant – had fully intended – to ring them while they were there, or to speak to my mother at least. But I couldn't. For some reason it all seemed too complicated. So I'll probably ring my mother tomorrow, and ask how it went, and whether they all had a good time – which I am sure they did; for how could they not have, unless they were thinking of me, that is, and my gloomy, shadowy presence had been clouding the bright sunshine of that happy, lovely place?

'Ah, well. I would be different if I could. If I could find the strength to change; to take another route; the one that they all wish me to take. But search in myself though I do, I cannot find it there. A larger Will – one with a great big capital letter – seems to be so much more powerfully at work in me than the one of my tiny, puny ego. And I have to face this; or I must do my best to face it, at least. I wish it were otherwise; and that is why I see so little of people just now. I don't want to face the looks of disapproval in their eyes; or the ones of pity and regret. That look is never there when John and Billy call; and certainly not when Joseph does either; which is why they now more or less constitute the entire round of my social world. For most of the time I am alone, and I *want* to be alone. I am not miserable. Vaguely sad, I suppose; wondering for much of the time why all this has come about; why I should be finding myself in this strange, this curious, situation . . . That business disturbed me the other night, on my way home: my actually wanting to *touch* that huge bloodstain on the pavement, half hoping, I have to confess, that it would still be wet, or be moist; and which is why I have written about it here, in this notebook. People – someone – ought to be told; ought to be made aware of this: mostly myself, I suppose.

'Does it spell danger, I wonder? Am I drifting towards something dark?: towards something evil, perhaps? If I am, I want to keep some kind of tag on it, in the hope (yes, I *do* have a degree of hope still left in that direction) that such self-consciousness, such self-awareness, might provide me with a turning point somewhere along the line, and that my will (the one with a lower-case letter) will find some new source of strength for bringing things back to order.

'Whatever, I now know that I can never be the things that I thought I could be. Of that, I am now sure. Having exposed a lie one cannot retell it; and I cannot possibly relive the lie of my previous existence, disturbing though the present one that I am encountering seems to be. Do I still laugh? Yes, sometimes, is the answer to that; when Joseph talks to me, for example, and goes on about the things that he does. Do I cry? No – quite *definitely not* – never. Do I love? Yes, I think I do – just a little. I still love my parents in a way: still love Betty. Still love my food too, alas – although that is a negative form of loving. But as for my wife, Jill, and as for my children – well, I feel fondness for them, yes; a real concern, in that I desire them to be well, to be happy; for the children to get on in life; for Jill to remarry, if she wants to, after the divorce, which I hope will be through soon. But not love. To say I feel a real love for them would be a lie, however much the reading of it here might offend whoever reads it.

'The point is, that writers are *meant* to tell the truth, the whole truth and nothing but it; which perhaps is why I am in the mess I am in today. Or is it? Ah – that is the big question, isn't it?: the sixty-four dollar one, as an American I knew in the war used to say. Are we what we are because of what we *were*? Are *all* our troubles of our own making? Somehow, I think not.

'May the gods bless you, Arnold, if they are lowering you into your grave just now, and if they are throwing a handful of dust on top of you. "Bon Voyage" – wherever it is you might be off to. Did they allow you to keep your hairpiece on, I wonder, when they placed you in your coffin? Did they allow you your usual splash of cologne behind your ears? (Why you didn't use a better-smelling one, I shall never understand.) A dusting of powder on your cheek; even a dab of rouge; to make you look your best? I shall miss you, Arnold; surprising though it is to find myself saying that. And so will your friends. Tears were shed on your behalf the morning you were found – by Billy. And real tears they were too: not the collective, conventional kind. The tears of one individual for another . . .

'Well, there will be few of those for me, I suspect, when my time comes. Somehow, I doubt that anyone will think that I have been worth them; or will have deserved them.'

At the foot of the page, Jason had added to the above piece of writing, this note – a kind of postscript; which said:

'I have been reading through this notebook; all that I have set down in it so far, and have come across something I wrote after my last visit to my parents. "The blood I fear to spill," I said, "and that I might yet *have* to spill, would poison and pollute that lovely world."

What blood? I ask; and why the word blood at all? My heart quakes at the idea that I should have used it, because I have read in Proust, who has wise thoughts about so many things, that although there are words we use that appear to lie, they in fact announce an approaching reality [*mais quelquefois l'avenir habite en nous sans que nous le sachions, et nos paroles qui croient mentir dessinent une réalité prochaine*].'

Soon after she had returned with her children to Cumbria, Jill was being questioned by her mother about their visit to the Callows.

'So it went well,' was her mother's opening remark; said with some tension in her voice, that seemed to suggest a half hidden hope that her daughter's reply would be a negative one.

'Yes, it did,' said Jill with her usual smile. 'Very. The Callows are nice people.'

'You have told me that before, Gillian. A lot of people are said to be that. But what did you *do*? If you did anything at all, that is.'

'Well, you are right about that, Mother. We didn't do very much – or *I* didn't. The children went for long walks – sometimes with Mr Callow. And one day we did go out. To Chawton; where Jane Austen lived and wrote. And that was lovely.'

'Oh, Jane Austen,' Jill's mother replied with a shudder. '*Her* trouble was that she never married. A touchy old spinster is what she was; and her books reek of it, it seems to me.'

'She was hardly old, Mother. And I think her books are full of love: for people. A very realistic love; but love all the same.'

'Well, I don't see it; but we've never agreed over our reading – have we, Gillian? You dislike Scott, for instance, and Kipling; both of whom are authors I admire . . . Did Jason ring while you were there, by the way? Or even call to see you at the house? – though I somehow doubt the latter.'

'He did neither, Mother. He neither came to the house nor spoke to us on the telephone.'

'You mean, you heard nothing from him whatsoever while you were there?'

'No, Mother.'

'Well, what sort of man *is* he, then? Who can't even ring and speak to his own children, when they are staying at his parents' house? He must have known that they would have liked to have heard from him: would have expected it, in fact.'

'Yes, it's true. But he didn't ring – no. Perhaps he was too shy to do so; or too timid.'

'Shy! Timid! Of his own wife? Of his own children? His own son and daughter? What nonsense that is, Gillian. Who ever heard of a father being too shy to telephone? It seems to me that something must be wrong. Does he have other interests, Gillian – that you know of, but haven't yet told me about?'

'Interests, Mother? Do you mean –?'

'Other women? Yes. Does he? Is there someone else that he is spending time with? That is usually the reason for men being negligent.'

'No, Mother, I am sure. There is no one. It is very likely that the mere idea of speaking to us upsets him. After all, he sees very little of us. Nothing of me, in fact; and the children only seldom.'

'Seldom! It is almost a year since *that* happened, Gillian. This really is most strange.'

'I admit that it is, Mother. I am aware of it.'

'Did his parents speak of him: say anything: ask questions?'

'Mrs Callow said she was worried, Mother; concerned. She said she thought Jason might be ill.'

'Good gracious! What with?'

'She didn't know. Not physically, she thought; but mentally, perhaps.'

'Mentally?'

'Yes.'

'But –'

'But what, Mother?'

'Well, I don't quite know what to say. I've never known anyone who was that. Has he seen a doctor – or whoever one sees for such things?'

'I don't know, Mother. I don't think so.'

'Well, perhaps you should act, Gillian: *do* something. Write and ask if it's true, perhaps.'

'Oh, no, Mother! I don't think that I –'

Gillians voice faded away to silence; and feeling agitated, she rose to leave the room. 'Excuse me, Mother', she said 'There are things that have to be seen to for supper; and the children will be home soon.'

Her mother looked at her; for once showing some real concern; as if, all of a sudden, something had touched her and affected her in a way that she was unused to. As if the idea of mental illness was something she had always kept at bay, as a concept to be feared.

'Gillian!' she called out, after her daughter had left her. 'Yes, Mother?' Jill called in reply.

'Oh, nothing,' her mother said, as she fiddled with her beads, and as her eyes dashed to and fro, watching the dancing flames of the fire. 'It's nothing, dear,' she added. 'It will keep until tomorrow.'

The next day, Jill received this letter from Jason:

Dear Jill,

I'm feeling horribly guilty about not having telephoned when you were in Hampshire. I meant to, but for some reason didn't – couldn't. So do please forgive me, and ask the children to do the same; and tell them that I'll have them down here in a while – once I am through this moment, which is a difficult one. At least you will be pleased to hear that I am writing. Not a book, but just thoughts – mostly about myself. Something I've never done.

Take care; and do buy yourself and the children something with the enclosed.

Jason

P.S. My regards please to your mother.

The day before this letter arrived, which was the day on

which it had been written and then posted, the world had seemed to Jason to be a dark and sorry place. He had attempted to voice his troubles, by going into them in his notebook; but for once, no words would form that were of value, and he had ended by deleting the entire entry; scribbling vigorously across it in large letters, 'I consider this to be rubbish.' And it had made Jason realise that he had come to some great obstacle of the mind: one that would be too difficult for him to surmount or to overcome; and that he really had no choice but to retreat from it and do nothing. Which was something easier said than done, of course, since to do nothing is something at which Westerners aren't skilled. And Jason knew only too well what danger there could be in such moments of inaction, when he could so easily become a victim of the listlessness from which he suffered.

And so, on account of the new consciousness that had become rooted in his mind, and that had been initiated, as he believed, by the purchasing of his new notebooks, he decided that he would attempt to stave off the danger he felt was threatening him, by doing something he had thought of doing, but that as yet he had not done; which was to consult the Chinese *Book of Changes*, or the *I Ching,* as it is also called, in the hope that its powers of wisdom and guidance would provide him with advice.

He knew little about the book, and had bought a copy of it only a few weeks before, having been given what had amounted to more or less a lecture about it from Joseph.

'I've been going into it,' Joseph had informed Jason one day, 'just to see if there's anything in it. Throwing the coins. Asking it questions.' And his conclusion had been that there was something 'bloody well uncanny about it . . . Of course, its language is odd,' he had said, 'curious. Or it is to me. Saying things like ten dozen pairs of tortoises cannot oppose this, and stuff like that. But you've got to think of it, I suppose, as answering you not so much in riddles as in images . . . Whatever,' he had said, 'you mustn't ask it vague, general questions about the state of the universe – that kind of thing. Always practical questions. Always about some action you wish to take, or that you *don't* wish to take, if that is how you are really feeling about it. It's about deeds, or so I gather; not ideas; built upon centuries of experience.'

And he had then explained to Jason in detail the method used for consulting the book. 'Forget yarrow sticks,' he had said, 'which is what it says you should use. Just use coins instead. Any three: of the same size and the same weight.' And he had then shown Jason what he must do in order to construct the two trigrams, as they are called, which constitute the particular variants of yin and yang – the opposites of the feminine and the masculine – upon which the book is based.

'Write your question down,' he had said, 'then sit facing north – I think that is what it says it has to be – and then throw the coins. Six times. Three heads make up a nine; and three tails a six; and anything else, of course, makes either a seven or an eight. This combination of numbers will then give you the chapter you have to look up – to get your answer, that is. *If* you get one,' he had added with a laugh, 'because you don't always, you know. Bloody subtle it is. If you ask the book something daft; something silly, I mean; it'll tell you that it doesn't suffer fools gladly, and will order you to consult the book again.'

So with this in mind, Jason approached the *I Ching* with caution, and in a sober manner: telling himself that he mustn't toy with it, or see it as being some form of mental trickery that might be used for purposes of diversion; and reminding himself, with all the deliberation that he could muster, of the dire need he had just then of some form of spiritual guidance; and of a kind that would be derived by many from their religion; or from the act of praying, perhaps; or today, possibly, from spending time with their analyst.

During the three years that he had been on his own – since Jill and the children had left him – it seemed as if all the energy of Jason's life had been directed towards this point; the one at which he had now arrived; and with what he saw as some huge mental barrier ahead of him, too thick for him to penetrate, too high for him to scale. But as he soon discovered, the difficulty proved to be that he was unable to formulate a question that he might put to the *I Ching*. Joseph had told him emphatically that it had to be practical questions, relating to deeds, so he could hardly ask it questions of a purely prophetic nature. 'It's not an oracle, exactly,' Joseph had said to him. And yet that was precisely what he felt a need of: some voice that would speak to him from the beyond; that would give him the relief of knowing what fate had lying in store for him. 'What I want to *know*,' he whispered, then half shouted, 'or what I *think* I want to know, is – whether –'

But here Jason paused, sensing that he was hovering on the brink of something so dark, something so dangerous, that everything in his conscious nature went against it. Yet the opposite side of him seemed to be attracting him towards it.

'Yes!' Jason now shouted – almost screamed, in fact; as he rose abruptly to his feet; and as he began to pace about the room, 'is whether I am wanting, *needing*, to kill! . . . Someone: something: myself perhaps!'

This scene took place at dead of night, when Jason was alone in the house – or he was as far as he could tell, since the ground floor of the building was lived in by an elderly couple who had a private entrance of their own, and who never used the main entrance-hall and staircase.

So he certainly felt alone, with Arnold no longer there, and with his apartment dark and empty. What Jason wasn't at all conscious of, however, was how powerful the rant of his voice could be, and he was astonished when his scream – for it had been nothing less than that – drew the attention of neighbours, and a few lights appeared in the windows of houses beyond the garden. In one of them, a bald-headed, pot-bellied man, with curious, frightened eyes, was drawing on a striped, silk dressing-gown; and in another, a pale, thin woman, with a knot of frizzy, unruly grey hair, stood staring into the darkness, wondering what the cause of the shriek she had heard had been. Then her eyes found the lighted windows of Jason's rooms, and the sight of Jason himself, pacing restlessly to and fro; and glancing out of the windows as he passed: scowling: wanting to shout across at her in the night that she should be minding her own business.

'Mind your own business!' he suddenly blurted out – pushing his head out of a partly open window: as if he was full of a kind of anger. After which, he slammed the window shut, then turned savagely into the room to find his notebook and to throw it into a corner; where he then stamped upon it; as if in revolt against the consciousness that it had come to represent.

Then, with a sudden, enormous surge of energy, he went out and down the staircase; leaving his door open behind him and switching the hall lights on as he went.

What he was wanting to do he didn't know; or where he was wanting to go – but when he reached the main entrance-door of the building he stopped, and fell panting against it.

For a while he clung there, with one hand on the handle of the door-lock, as if preparing to race out into the street; but then, as quickly as it had arisen, the anger in him subsided; and almost blindly, he groped for a heavy metal bolt that was seldom used, and thrusting it vigorously upwards, double-locked himself in.

With his face pressed tightly against the door, Jason waited for the quick throb of his breathing to lessen. Then he turned to face the empty hallway, and the flight of stairs he had climbed so often. And as he did so, the memory came to him of Arnold's curious, ginger-wigged figure; accompanied by the sharp sound of his high-pitched, voice; asking him if he had perhaps been out again with his 'arty-tarty' friends. And Jason knew then that the point of crisis in him had passed, and that he had not done whatever it was that he might have done that night; and with slow, deliberate steps he returned cautiously to his rooms.

XIII

IT WAS MORE than a week before Jason was able to relate to what had happened to him that night.

'And even now I am finding it difficult,' he said, as he began to write of it in his notebook. 'To have been in the grips of something so negative and so much larger than myself. To have been so compelled – so driven towards an action that I knew so surely must be destructive; and that made me want to stamp out, made me want to obliterate, any awareness I might have of it. Even to stamp upon this book of mine in which I am writing now, and which, I can say quite truthfully, I have come to treasure: because what has been said in it means that I am still able to "read" my life, and so acquire for it some meaning.

'And that is everything, isn't it? to give one's life that. People, it seems to me – men – women – will forgo everything for the sake of it. They may not think that they will. They may tell themselves that sex and money come first in the natural order of things, but the fact is that they don't. The religious instinct, if one speaks about it in the very broadest sense, is what comes first for us – is what counts most for us, because that is what we would seem to be here for on this earth, to give meaning to our lives, and through that to the world.

'Anyway, it is now almost two weeks since I passed through what must surely have been the most difficult moment of my life; when, without knowing why, I felt drawn towards so dark, so utterly negative a deed that I can hardly bring myself to think of it – let alone to write about it here, as I am attempting to do, now, on this page. And the curious thing is that there has been no focus, no object, upon which this urge has been projected. It is not as if I have had negative desires in me that have been directed towards people; or towards things, or animals even – that exist outside myself. And yet I do know (oh dear! I can hardly write this down) – I do realise, that blood is involved; because the sight of blood, the smell, the touch of it, is now so very present in my mind; and is always there: is always lurking, hovering – threatening. Not right now. Not as I am writing this; for it is only when I write that it goes away; whenever I am making myself conscious of it in a heightened sense, which one *can* do through the use of words. And to be absolutely accurate in my expression, and to tell an exact truth of the 'nothing but' variety, it – the awareness of blood – has certainly been less present in me during the past week or so, less than it has for quite a while; for quite a few months, perhaps.

'I won't say – I won't think – that the crisis I experienced, and that ended with my locking myself in – or with my *bolting* myself in – has brought me out of danger. I am not so stupid as to imagine that that perhaps could be the case. For at the end of each day the night must always return, and I know that that must be true of things of the mind; although quite how I know it I am uncertain.

'Whatever, to report further on my condition . . . I have now trimmed my beard more carefully than I had been doing and have trimmed my hair as well – although not yet gone to the barber as I need to do and as I ought to have done. I have even discarded the old, striped scarf I had taken to wearing, and I have ventured out, when I *have* ventured out, without the pair of thick winter mittens I had taken to putting on, and that I had been keeping on for most of each day, even though the weather has been so mild for what is now the end of October.

'And – yes – what has been of significance to me is that I have told my wife, Jill, that I *might* have the children here at Christmas. Not "for" Christmas, I didn't say that; but during their holidays. I even rang to tell her this. Even spoke to her mother about it, who happened to answer the call, and who was at first extremely cold, but then less so. And Jill, when I spoke to her, seemed so pleased – because, she said, the children would be that; because they are constantly asking after me and are wanting to come and see me.

'Yes, that was significant, certainly. But did it make me feel closer to my family: make me feel more fond of them?, is a question I need to ask. And the answer that anyone reading this will be looking for is that it did, I suppose. But the truth I am afraid to say is almost the opposite . . . Yes, I do feel more human for it, if you like; and I do feel relieved to know that to a small extent I have been able to fit in more with society's collective modes of behaviour. But it would be a lie to say that I have been drawn closer to either my children or my wife.

'The truth that wants to come out is this – that I no longer wish to feel close to *anyone*, not in any intimate sense; and that I either do not want that form of tie, that form of closeness, or that I fear it. *Or* (which is very possible, I suppose), that I fear *for* anyone who might become involved with me, and so grow close to me. Which is why, no doubt, that on certain days and at certain times, I still walk the streets alone: still drawing close to people in the shops; half wanting to feel their warmth, to smell their presence. Because they are people I do not know and shall *never* know, and therefore the question of any more intimate form of closeness is something I do not have to consider.

'Now, some further notes on my condition . . .

'I am eating and drinking less – and that's a good thing as well, because it means I have lost a little weight. Not much, but a little. And I have even telephoned my publisher and half apologised to him in case he had been offended by what I had said to him when we last spoke. And I am missing my landlord, of course – although why I say "of course", I really don't know, since it is hardly something I would have said when he was alive. His must be a very pervading spirit, for it is ever present, here in this house; in its hallway and on its stairs; and there is scarcely a day goes by when I do not hear his high-pitched voice and chatter . . . Also – and this is important to me, for some reason that I don't think I can explain – I've seen John and Billy twice during the past ten days. On the first occasion, I invited them here for a drink, with the idea that if things happened to go well, I would then invite them out for supper.

'They arrived in their suits; freshly scrubbed: their ties neatly knotted; and to begin with were stiff and formal, which made it difficult for me to relate to them. They kept glancing about the room; kept looking at my books; at my letters; at my clothes – which, as usual, were strewn across the backs of various pieces of furniture. But gradually, helped by a few drinks, they became quite talkative, and we enjoyed each other's company a lot.

'The second time we met, they insisted that I visit them at their flat – which is very small, and which is tucked beneath the heavy mansard roof of a Victorian mansion in South Kensington. And there they were more relaxed, and prepared a much better meal for me than I had provided for them; when, as I had hoped that we would, we had eaten out at a local restaurant.

'John knows and reads a lot – far more than I had imagined; and Billy, who is delightfully curious, asks a lot of questions. However, the thing that really surprised me was that they quarrelled. Why had I not expected that, I wonder? Why should not two men who live together quarrel? I was surprised to find that I had never imagined such a thing. Anyhow, they did – and it was all over a friend of Billy's called Damien, or something; who John said was no good, and someone he thought Billy ought not to be seeing.

'"He's no good," John had said. "I know. He's just negative" – and then had said no more; which, for a while, made Billy sulk.

'But it wasn't for long, and we were then able to enjoy ourselves in much the same way that I am able to enjoy myself when I am with Joseph – who has been out of London, by the way. Not on holiday (that is something in which he never indulges – mainly because he can't afford it), but because his father has been ill – dying, I think he said he was – so I've not seen anything of him, of Joseph, for some time, and there has been none of his Epistles to the Ignorant, as a result.

'All in all then, life has been just a little sweeter of late: just a little more normal, I suppose I have to call it, much as I dislike using that word.

'Now, some plans I am making for myself . . .

'I have considered – indeed, am still considering – going to see a doctor, or to see a psychiatrist, rather; or is it an analyst? to find out if there is anything that can be done to help me rid myself of my troubles. But the will to take that step has been lacking . . . And *that* is what tells me that my difficulties are not yet over. That even now; even when there are at least signs of some improvement at last, I still lack the will to act in that particular way: to go to see someone who would at least tell me what might be wrong with me – if something *is* wrong with me that is put-rightable, that is. But I half fear, half know, that whoever I go to see I shall be sent packing: shall be told that mine is a case of the "better *not* to know than to know" variety – which I understand is a thing that does exist; and that I shall simply have to put up with (and manage to somehow make some kind of peace with) this monster that inhabits me.

'Concerning the time of year . . .

'November is now not far away. The trees in the parks have already shed great numbers of their leaves, and the city has taken on that curious moment of pause that it always manages to achieve before the final weeks that lead up to Christmas. People who have gardens, or who have balconies, have been pulling up their faded, summer plants – or what is left of them – and turning over the earth, and putting in the daffodil bulbs and crocus bulbs and snowdrops. Do I have any such bulbs that I might plant in my own mind? – to help see me through the wintry months ahead? Not really. Not even the thought that I might be having the children here for a while. Nor, for that matter, does the idea of going down to Hampshire to see my parents, which I have arranged to do before the end of the month.

'No, there is *nothing*, it seems, that I can safely count upon as being of comfort to me; and I have no choice it would appear but to accept that. What is worrying me, and has been for some days, is that I have been hearing things inside my head – words, that is, that have kept repeating themselves. I have no idea of where they come from or who wrote them – they could even be a translation by the sound of them – but they speak fearsomely and with irony about the "mighty justice of the gods" – who, they constantly say to me –

> Will lead us to the edge of some abyss,
> Then cause us to commit great crimes
> For which they will not pardon us.'

At the foot of the page Jason had added the following note:

'I am glad to have written what I have written. To some, self-ignorance may be bliss, but to me, it is fast becoming the opposite.'

PART FOUR

XIV

THE LADY WHO lived opposite – that is to say, who lived in the house across the street from the one in which Jason lived – was not, as Arnold had imagined she might be, the keeper of some exclusive, upper-class brothel; she was the widow of a wealthy, titled stockbroker, who called herself, incorrectly, Lady Cynthia Barron. And as for the various men that Arnold had commented upon, and that he had seen calling at her door, these were either Lady Cynthia's two brothers, both of whom were as plump and pink as Lady Cynthia was herself, or it would have been a rather dashing figure by the name of Captain Frederick Smythe, who was Lady Cynthia's lover.

In the years before the war, 'Captain Smythe', as Lady Cynthia called him (for even in private she seldom used his Christian name), had been an officer in the army; and during the war itself, was said to have done secret work for 'Intelligence'; for which he was admirably suited, since he was devious and rather clever.

Lady Cynthia thought the world of him, however, and was always showing him off to her circle of friends – announcing to dinner guests as they arrived that 'Captain Smythe is going to be here and it's going to be fun' – which, indeed, it usually was; for between them, they generated a breezy air of excitement; and one that suggested to people (although this was seldom brought to the very forefront of their minds) that once they had left, and the party was over, fun would take place of a quite different kind.

'Naughty stuff,' Lady Cynthia might say, if she happened to meet a close friend of hers the next day; followed by a quick wobble of her cheeks, and then by a similar one of her hat (if the meeting took place in the street, that is); and also with a swing of the long, free-flowing clothes that she wore, and that were usually in different shades of blue; and that duly matched, in a remarkably subtle way, the soft water-blues of her eyes; that were ever adrift and afloat in the shifting seas of her too heavily powdered features.

Unlike the other women in her circle, whose main pastime was playing bridge, the interesting thing about Lady Cynthia was the real passion she had for the opera; and whenever Captain Smythe came to spend the night with her, he had grown accustomed to the idea that before they retired to bed, she would play long stretches of Wagner to him on her record player: and this, he had come to understand, was meant to prepare for the events that followed. And it could have been that Lady Cynthia had things in mind for her lover for which he was unprepared, for what he didn't know was that the night attire she wore, and that so cleverly veiled and subtly flattered the sweeping curves of her over-large figure, had been modelled upon a stage-costume she had once seen at Covent Garden, worn by the heroine of *Lohengrin*; in which, of course, the famous 'Wedding March' is played.

However, if the 'thing' about Lady Cynthia was the passion she had for opera, then the thing about Captain Smythe was the fierce passion he had for old motor cars – fast, noisy ones in particular; and it had been much remarked upon in the area that his frequent arrivals at the house – and his departures from it as well – were accompanied by the snarls and roars of these old cars of his: sometimes, if he was anxious to get away, in the very early hours of the morning.

'Yes, I *know* they are loud,' Lady Cynthia had once answered in his defence, 'but there it is, he loves them . . . Besides,' she had added, 'he has such verve, such vivacity' – which, on the whole, was true.

What Lady Cynthia rarely spoke about, however, was her lover's lack of dependability, in that she could never be sure whether he would keep his appointments with her or not; and when someone had once dared to suggest to her that the cause of this might be that he had other ladies to visit, she had spoken curtly in reply, saying that what the Captain did was his own business. 'And in any case,' she had added haughtily, 'he is perfectly delightful, and a splendid lover as well.'

In the sense that they had not been introduced to each other, Arnold and Lady Cynthia had never met; but if he had been sufficiently aware of her to have had ideas about who she might be, then she had been equally so of him. For in much the same way that Arnold had spoken about his neighbour as being 'That woman who lives opposite, and who wears long strings of pearls and enormous, floppy blue hats', so she, when speaking of him, would describe him as 'That funny old thing who lives across the road from me, and who wears what I am convinced is an ill-fitting, ginger wig'; which she had then embellished with, 'Exactly *who* he is, I don't know; and I don't know that I *want* to know; much as he has an unusual looking woman-friend, that I see with him at times; who wears bright red lipstick, and dumpy, narrow-brimmed hats; and who is rather smart, I think; if a little too masculine, perhaps, for my idea of a woman.'

'But you know, my dear,' she had gone on, 'she *is* very interesting, I find; and so is he, perhaps. But then, we do have interesting people here in Chelsea, you know. We always have had. There is nothing dull or suburban here . . . Have you seen that wicked Max Adrian, in the revue at the Royal Court, by the way? He is extraordinary in it, I am told; and the whole thing so smart and so sophisticated; which accounts, of course, for its success.'

All of which is to show that Lady Cynthia was much more conscious of her neighbour than she gave the impression of being on the surface; and although when encountering each other in the street, they would eye each other guardedly, as if they might be passing ships in the night, watching the distance between them with caution, she would often look down from her bedroom window, to see who might be arriving at his door, and who might be departing from it as well; which meant that she was also aware of Jason – who in recent months had been disturbing her, on account of his appearance: due to the two topcoats he'd taken to wearing, one worn over the other; and to the frayed, striped scarf that he kept wrapped around his neck; and (this had become the latest addition), the pair of thick, woollen mittens that he had taken to wearing as well, in what was still quite mild, autumnal weather.

On account of the keen ear that she had for local gossip, Lady Cynthia had learned that Jason was a writer, and this fascinated her, much as she was no real lover of books and words. 'Mind you,' she had remarked to someone one day, 'what *sort* of thing he writes I have no idea; but he's become quite a figure here of late. Something of a sight, if you like. He's glowered at me at times, when he's seen me in the street. Why, I can't think . . . Captain Smythe believes that something is wrong with him – mentally; and told me that when he had once asked him to give his car a push, he just hadn't answered. Just stared at him, he said – and had then walked on . . . Ah, well,' she had added, 'it takes a lot to make a world – all sorts; and I don't believe that he really *means* to be rude, because there is kindness in his eyes, and that is how I always judge people – by their looks . . . Mind you,' she said again, 'I have *heard* that he has been separated from his wife for quite a while; and that there is to be a divorce; so my suspicion is that he is unsettled, and that he is probably distressed by that.'

Thus the talk and chatter of the neighbourhood wove and rewove its web, constructing in the minds of those who lived there a picture of its rich and varied character. And who knows how many such images were formed and re-formed each day, passing from one small group to another. Images that had been based upon mere surface impressions, of course, and that therefore lacked the depth and fullness of any more perceptive kind of knowledge. And certainly no one who lived in the area at that time had any real sense of Jason's troubles. Not even Joseph, who saw his friend quite frequently, was fully conscious of the fact that Jason was in the grips of mental disturbances that were of an unusually troublesome kind; and that even if the symptoms of that illness were now temporarily in abeyance, the illness itself still threatened; making him think that life for him was too unstable, and that he would find no real peace for himself until some further crisis had passed; and then perhaps another; knowing as he did that the self-consciousness he had been nurturing (and that was partly due, he had come to believe, to his having purchased those new notebooks) was not yet strong; and that it was as yet incapable of providing him with the defences he was seeking, against those disturbing impersonal actions that from time to time took hold of him and would threaten to possess him.

In view of the fact that she knew quite a considerable amount about what went on in the streets and houses around her, it was odd that Lady Cynthia hadn't been told of Arnold's death. She had sensed a change, however, because she had seen such a lot less of Lottie of late; and had noticed that the times of her visits were different. For she now spent a few hours at the house each morning, rather than in the later part of the day, which was when she had usually called to see Arnold (ignoring her night-time visits, that is). And there was another change of which Lady Cynthia had now become aware, that had nothing to do with Arnold's death (other than the coincidence of its timing); which was that, from a distance, at least (for of late she had only observed him from her window, not passed him in the street), it seemed that Jason was looking less ragged and unkempt. He was wearing no scarf, she had noticed, and no mittens; and it looked as if his hair and beard had been trimmed.

Whether or not she had found some means of protecting herself from hearing the news that Arnold had died, is a question one might well ask; for the subject of death and dying was one she seldom gave time to, and that she usually kept banished from her mind. And if she found herself alone of an evening, and without company, then she would suppress any reflective thoughts that might come to her regarding the impermanence of life, by busying herself with her letters, or by tidying a drawer, perhaps; or by just telephoning her friends. Which meant that when she did eventually hear of Arnold's death, she showed no reaction to it whatsoever. 'Poor man,' was all she had muttered, and had then diverted the conversation.

For to Lady Cynthia, the most important thing in life was to be sure she kept abreast of things, and to be ever pressing on. She didn't exactly sing each morning in her bath, but she certainly expected to step from it in a mood of optimism and hope; and if the weather happened to be fine, then there was nothing that provided her with more pleasure than to have slipped on one of the long flowing housegowns she wore; and to be at one of her bedroom's sunlit windows, seeing to her nails or to her hair; and to be catching a glimpse beyond the rooftops of the morning's clear, blue sky; and to be thinking to herself that, in certain ways, she was but a reflection of all this; of the bright, cheerful sky, and of the first hopeful hours of the day; and to be seeing herself as a portrait that had been painted in nothing but pinks and blues and gold; and as being of someone who is full of love and benevolence, and of the proverbial milk of human kindness.

XV

WHEN JOSEPH MALLORY returned to London from the country, he immediately rang Jason, in order to arrange for them to meet. But it was not with his customary intention – the one of wanting to use his friend as a kind of testing-ground for his ideas – it was because his father had just died, and he needed to speak to someone about it.

'Yes,' he said, when he came to see Jason that same day, and at about five in the afternoon, 'it happened just a few hours after I arrived. I knew he was seriously ill, of course – we all did; my sisters; my mother – but none of us expected him to be gone *that* bloody quickly.'

'What do you make of it – eh – Jason?' he had continued. 'This business of dying, and of our not being able to see what's beyond it – what's on the other side of it. . . It's a bit of a "con", I think – don't you? – to be pushed into this life, all fitted out with the full works of the body, and all that goes with it – and then, before you can say Jack fucking Robinson, you're being whisked away. Off. To where? No one bloody well knows . . . Watching my father die like that – watching him laughing and chatting, as if nothing was wrong; and then, the next moment, collapsing exhausted upon his pillow, gasping for breath; and then, that was it, he had gone – made me angry . . . I mean, he hadn't had much of a life, poor sod. Worked hard, just to keep on top of things; and then – bang! – he's knocked for a six: gone for a bloody Burton.'

'You were fond of him, Joe,' Jason stated, noticing how emotional his friend had become; and in such a different way from when he would be voicing his ideas.

'Yes. I suppose I was,' Joseph replied, clenching his jaw, and causing his neck muscles to tighten, 'though we never showed much affection towards each other; except, perhaps, through the arguments we had, which might have been *our* way of expressing it I suppose . . . 'He was very "left", Jason – you know. A real socialist. Not sceptical about politics, as I am. He still believed – in spite of the war, I mean – that some kind of fairness was possible: that decent people living decently, working hard – would get their rewards. And he'd clung on to that . . . We'd almost scrap at times about things like that. And my being a painter didn't make things easier for him, I'm afraid. My not having a "proper job", as he called it – that was a real bother to him. My mother – she was the supportive one; who thought that what I was doing was worthwhile – was honourable, if you like. But there, when it comes to spiritual matters, women can be like that – can't they? They say it's the women who're the real visionaries; who see the new things first. But few of them will voice it publicly. They'll see it, but then they'll want to smother it; with their conservatism; to do with their motherhood, I suppose – their need for stability and so on; and to cling to the status quo . . . I don't know if there's any truth in that idea, but there could be, I guess . . . Was *your* mother supportive, Jason?'

'Oh yes, she *was*,' Jason answered with a quick laugh, 'and she still is. She still believes in my work. Still believes in *me*, for that matter; even if I no longer do myself.'

'Jason! What the fuck are you *saying*?' exclaimed Joseph,

never having heard his friend express himself in this way before, and showing real attention and concern.

'I'm saying what I've just said to you, Joe; that I've told a lie, and that I've been telling it all my life. Not just through my work, Joe. Through my marriage, my children, my –'

'Oh, *bollocks*, Jason! How can you *say* that? How can you *speak* like that? You're a bloody good writer, Jason, and you damn well *know* that you are; and people think you are too. The people who read you and so on: the people who buy your books; the people who publish them.'

Jason didn't answer this. Instead, he went to refill their glasses.

'Look, Jason,' said Joseph, 'we'd better go out, I think. Go to a pub or something. Get ourselves a bite to eat . . . You've been too shut up with yourself, it seems to me. You've lost weight, Jason, you know. Quite a lot. Have you been eating properly?'

'Yes, you're right, Joe – we'll go out,' Jason replied, not answering Joseph's question. 'And I'll invite you,' he added, lifting up the two glasses he was carrying, as if he was making a public toast. 'Yes,' he repeated, his eyes suddenly turning inward, and half nodding to the air.

'There's no need,' Joseph replied, noticing the change in Jason's appearance, as if some cloud had just passed over him. 'I've got money on me for once. Cash. Given to me by my mother . . . There was a lot in the house, she said, and my father wanted me to have it. But nothing about it to my sisters, she said.'

Jason smiled. 'I wish I had had a sister, Joe. It's something I've wished for all my life.'

'And my wish has been the opposite,' said Joe, 'to have had a brother.'

'Well then, we've both wished for something we couldn't have,' said Jason, 'that was denied to us.'

For a while, the two men sipped their drinks in silence, in what, with the daylight now having failed, had become a darkened room; beyond the windows of which the deep night sky stretched clear towards the river, from where a brisk wind had struck up, that was driving towards the streets and houses with force; whipping dead leaves from the trees that line the embankment, and causing them to flutter aimlessly against window panes, or to scutter hurriedly towards the shelter of garden walls; or to fall flat and lifeless, spreadeagled upon the pavements.

'It's from the south-west,' said Jason, hearing the sudden whine of the wind, and so breaking the spell of silence.

'Yes,' said Joseph, 'but at least there'll be no frost.'

Again the two friends fell silent. Which was quite an event for them, since Joseph was so inclined to fill whatever time they shared with talk. Then Jason rose from his chair to switch on a table lamp, placed close to where they were sitting.

'Joe, it's good to see you,' Jason said, looking down at his friend.

'And to see you, Jason,' said Joseph, a little embarrassed.

'Shall we go then?' asked Jason, now feeling embarrassed himself. 'I don't know about you, Joe, but I'm famished.'

Without giving a thought to what he was doing, Jason moved towards a chair at the back of the room, and went to collect from it the old, striped scarf that he had worn until a few weeks ago: but as he stooped to pick it up, he was reminded of the attempts that he had been making to achieve a platform for himself, that he hoped would be firm and steady; and upon which, as he had begun to imagine it, he might at last be able to rest.

'Jason! It's not cold,' Joseph almost shouted at him, 'You won't *need* a scarf.'

'No?' said Jason, turning to look at his friend with a distant expression on his face; and as if the attraction of the scarf had suddenly removed him from the world, and from all that was around him.

'*No*,' replied Joseph, firmly, noticing Jason's glassy stare. 'You hardly need a coat, Jason, let alone a scarf.'

'Oh,' said Jason, sounding confused. 'Well, I'll just take a coat then . . . Better do that, I think. It's November. It's going to be Guy Fawkes night next week.'

'Christ! So it is!' said Joseph, as he quickly emptied his glass, and as he rose to join Jason at the door. 'There'll be bonfires in all the bloody gardens again. Smoke too; fog, probably – if the weather turns. Or even smog, perhaps.'

'Joe? Can I say something?' Jason then asked, once Joseph had crossed the room to join him and they were both ready to leave. 'Can I tell you something?'

Joseph looked nervously at his friend, sensing that he was about to hear something for which he was unprepared.

'Yes, Jason – what is it?' he answered a little sharply, showing that he didn't much care to hear whatever Jason might have to say.

'Joe,' Jason repeated, 'if – if anything were to happen to me; like what has just happened to your father, I mean; I want you to know that I've mentioned you in my will. You're aware, I think, that my grandfather left me money, and I want you to have some of it . . . Not a really large amount, because of Jill and the children, of course – but something. And I've done that because – well, because I've valued you; valued knowing you, and that you've been a real friend.'

'Oh, for fuck's *sake*,' said Joseph, his face reddening, and unable to cope with the flush of emotion that Jason's words had released. 'Stop bloody well *talking* like that – will you, Jason? You're not going to kick the bucket yet, you know. Now – come on: let's go out and eat. We've been bloody well drinking too much – that's what it is; and on empty stomachs as well. Now, that's enough of it, Jason – do you hear? All this talk about bloody wills and stuff – and dying.'

Jason smiled and patted his friend lightly upon the shoulder, then gave a quick, boyish laugh.

'You're right, Joe,' he said, 'as usual'; and with that, flicked on a switch at the head of the staircase and flooded the stairwell with light. Then, with a sudden rise in their spirits and a gradual quickening of their steps, the two friends made their way down.

As the days passed and as November drew to a close, Jason's stability strengthened, and he began to feel a little pleased with himself. Not hopeful (he knew he must not be that), but as Joseph had said to him, he had lost some weight, so he felt more in control of himself than he had done for more than a year. He had been away – to Hampshire – to see his parents; and the visit had pleased him: his mother commenting upon how well he looked – 'You're more your old self, Jason,' she had said – and Betty amusing him with the remarks she had made about the book she was currently reading – and which, of all books, happened to be Emily Brontë's *Wuthering Heights*.

'Fancy a young woman writing a book like that,' had been her comment. 'Where on earth did such a thing come from, I wonder? . . . I mean, that Heathcliff man, I can't make him out. Such a figure, he is. He's more the devil than anything else, it seems to me. And poor Cathy, ending up in the grave like that, and with him pouncing down on top of her . . . Well, it's a work of the imagination, I suppose; and who can tell what goes on inside another person's head. Have you read it, Jason?' she asked.

'Yes, of course I have,' answered Jason with a smile. 'It's a classic, Betty.'

'Well, it must be,' Betty replied, 'because it's such a story, and I could hardly put it down. Do you think *you* could write something like that, Jason?'

Jason laughed and said that he hardly thought that possible.

'Well, it would be a good thing if you could,' was Betty's harsh reply. 'All that passion. *That's* what makes a book tick.'

Jason had said nothing to this, since what his mind was so taken up with just then was the composing of a poem. He had been reflecting upon his 'story', as he thought of it – the one that he had avoided all his life and that he was now doing his best to face and to make real – and his thoughts had finally crystallised in a few lines about Coriolanus, which was the subject Joseph had spoken about a while ago, and in the story of which he had seen a reflection of himself. And soon after returning to London from the country, he had decided to write this poem in his notebook; and then to add beneath it a few reflections upon why he had written it, and about what the poem meant to him.

Here is a copy of the poem; and following it, the relevant extract from Jason's notebook.

> A great deal has been written on
>   the life of Coriolanus
> But the manner of his death remains
>   mysterious and unknown
> Plutarch, for instance, says that he
>   was killed by Volscian soldiers;
> Others, that he was murdered by
>   the Volscian leader's sword:
> But Livy, who quotes Fabius as the
>   earliest authority,

Makes claims for his continuing to
    live on in lonely exile;
A sad, perhaps embittered, somewhat
    cautionary old man.

'I have written this poem over the past few weeks, allowing it to form gradually in my mind, and needing to have something upon which to focus. For I am still feeling nervous about myself; wondering who I am exactly, and where I might be going. Like Coriolanus, I have turned my back upon my former life – upon my public life, as one might speak of it; and which includes the one I led with my family – meaning, with my wife and my two children. And I have also had strong feelings of disgust concerning my work – my writing – knowing how shallow it is and intellectual in the wrong way. For never in my work have I touched any fire – any real passion, as Betty speaks of it. My books have been admired by many for their style, their skill; but they have been cold pieces of writing, it seems to me, and I have gradually become aware of it. Some writers – some critics – have described my books as being "cool", and have used that word as a form of compliment; as though to have kept one's distance from whatever lies beneath the surface of life should be counted a virtue; but I have not been able to accept that idea.

'So what *is* my real story, I wonder? Am I, like Coriolanus, destined to become some kind of recluse? Someone who can no longer cope with wordly things, and who is forced, as he was, to enter some peculiar form of exile?

'The idea of such a thing is unpleasant to me, yet that could be the truth of what I am destined to become. For days now – no, for weeks – my life has been more calm and ordered than it has been for quite some time. I have had no sudden fits of depression; have felt no need to wander the streets at night – or even to wander them during the daytime – and I have done my best to keep in touch with people. I have even made tentative arrangements for Christmas; planning to have the children here; and thinking of presents I might buy them in the immediate weeks ahead. Yet I still feel anxious. Still feel that I do not know what lies in store for me. I wish – oh, *how* I wish! – that I could grasp it; could gain some knowledge of it; could get just a glimpse of my direction.

'I have been reading a lot – more than I ever did – and Joseph has come to spend time with me quite regularly; either here, or I have met him out at our local pub. And from time to time I have seen John and Billy as well; which means that on the surface at least, all has seemed calm and almost serene. But I know from experience that the monster that inhabits me has still not gone away: that it is still there: that it still waits, watches, still listens.

'Sometimes, I think that I should attempt to confront this thing of darkness: should call its bluff, perhaps: provoke it: take actions that are dangerous and that would challenge both it and myself. Just to see. Just to test my story. But something holds me back – stops me from doing that – as if it might provoke a fight, some kind of battle, in which I would be the loser.

'So I plod on; praying that with time my will will strengthen; and that if I can sustain the tension for long enough, the dangers will go away, and I shall begin to feel at least some modicum of security and achieve a point of rest.

'Am I frightened? Yes, perhaps I am. Am I hiding

my fright? Perhaps that too. Perhaps I've been pushing things under the carpet, or burying my head in sand, if either of those are suitable expressions to use. But what else can I do?

'Whatever, I can say this – can write it down here – that if, as I go on, I begin to learn that a retreat from life is the only truthful way for me, then I will do my best to accept it – without grumbles, quarrels or resentments. *Nothing but the truth*, is what I am asking of myself. To know as much as I can, as much as I am *allowed* to know, of who or what I am.

'Because I have learned of it from books, I know that there are faulty structures of the mind, and I have read of what is termed a psychotic state; something latent in the mind, which, when touched upon, I gather, or when activated in some way (as it can be by an excess of self-consciousness, I presume) can explode; and in a manner similar, I suspect, to when I was shouting from my window those few weeks ago, and frightening the people who live opposite; after which, I trampled upon this notebook of mine, then raced madly down the stairs, driven to do I know not what.

'So perhaps a firm steeling of the nerves, and a persistent avoidance of any such murky areas of the mind, is what is best for me. Something tells me – by which I mean that this is a judgement based only upon instinct – that even if I did go to see a doctor (or an analyst, rather) I would only be told what I have just said; and it could be that this is what I have to face: to be continually watchful, guarded, cautious.

'Well, whatever will be will be; and only time, I fear, will be the revealer of what it is.'

XVI

AS EVERYONE WHO lives in England knows, once November has passed and the year at last moves towards Christmas, there is a change that takes place in both the spiritual as well as the physical climate of the country. People become more cheerful – perhaps because they have come to accept the darkness of winter; its long nights; its occasional storms and heavy rain; the bitter winds that can blow. There is seldom much frost or snow: that is usually delayed until the New Year. And certainly in London, there is a sudden atmosphere of excited busyness and cheer. People think of nothing but the presents they are going to buy for the Christmas festival; of the new clothes they might indulge in; of what they might wear to this or that party; and the murky days of November are thrust aside.

As for December's weather – that too can be different. It can be cold – sometimes extremely so – but there can also be days that are bright and sunny – with high clouds piled up against the pale silver-blues of the sky – and that seem to speak of a springtime that will come; bursting through with such sudden force out of the dark months that lie behind it.

It was on such a day as this that Lilian Callow chose to inspect her garden, to see that everything there was in order; noting, as she did so, that the holly trees were thick with berries (a sign, she had been told, that the winter would be severe); but which, nonetheless, pleased her, thinking as she did that she would have plenty of sparkling sprigs to bring indoors, and that would help her to cheer and liven the house and to make it welcoming for the family. For Jason, that is, who had promised to be there, and for his brother Jeremy and his wife and their two children.

There was no wind, but the temperature was low; and Lilian was wrapped warmly in a fleece-lined sheepskin jacket. But as she stooped to lift the stem of a rose that had recently been pruned, and that had broken free of the wooden trellis upon which it had been trained to climb, she felt on her back at least a little of the sun's warmth.

Pausing in her task, Lilian turned to look at what she still thought of as her father's house, and was pleased by the sight of smoke rising steadily from its chimneys; knowing this meant that Betty had made up the fires and that the house would soon be warm.

'Lilian!' her husband called out, who had come to a window to find her. 'It's the phone.'

'The what?' she asked, not quite hearing what he had said.

'The phone, dear. It's Jason.'

Picking up a garden trug that she had left close to where she was working, Lilian turned to make a sign to her husband that she would come in to take the call; and wondered at the same time why Jason should have rung at such an unusual hour, which was shortly after breakfast.

'But Jason, why at *this* time of day?' she asked her son cheerfully. 'It's so *early*!'

'Oh – no special reason,' was Jason's reply. 'I just felt a need to speak to you, and to ask about presents.'

'Presents, dear?'

'Yes. For Christmas. What to buy father, for instance.'

'Oh, my!' exclaimed Lilian with relief; expressing how pleased she was that Jason had no more serious reason for calling. 'I don't know. I'll have to think . . . Books? No — because he's always so fussy and wants such particular ones. So what then? Well, a pair of braces, perhaps – good ones; with leather straps or whatever you call them, that go over the buttons.'

'Well, *that's* not much of a present,' said Jason with a chuckle.

'Yes, dear. I know it's not; but it *is* what he wants.'

'Then I'll get both. Braces and a book; if you could just find out what kind of book he would like.'

'Well, I can. Yes – I will.'

'And you, Mother? What would you like?'

'Me? Oh, perfume, perhaps – will that do? Not that I use it much . . . Something subtle.'

'Shall I get the usual, then?' said Jason, knowing his mother's taste.

'Yes, yes,' she replied, 'that would be lovely.'

There was then a brief pause in the conversation, before Lilian asked a little nervously if Jason was well.

'Are you?' she had added to her question.

'I am – yes: quite.'

'Better than you have been, I mean? Even than you were when you came here to us last?'

'I think I am – yes. It comes and goes.'

Again there was a pause, before Lilian risked saying,

'What does, Jason, dear? What comes and goes?'

'Oh, my troubles.'

'You've never really spoken about them, Jason, you know: to us: to your father and myself. We've seen that something has been wrong, but haven't quite liked to ask what it might be.'

'And I am glad you haven't, Mother,' said Jason, 'because even now I can't speak about it; can't define it. I am just

168

unwell at times — that is all I can say. Mentally, I mean. There is nothing physically wrong with me.'

'Then shouldn't you see someone about it, Jason? Being on your own can't be good for you. Shouldn't you see a doctor to find out what might be wrong?'

'I have thought of it, Mother, and will if I feel I must. But for the moment —'

'For the moment what, Jason?'

'For the moment I can manage, I think, since I do feel rather better than I did: and I *look* better too, I am told.'

'Oh, Jason! I am so *glad* that you rang,' Lilian suddenly blurted out. 'I can't tell you, Jason, how much we are looking forward to Christmas, and to us all being here together . . . If only Jill and the children could have been here as well . . . But there it is. We've gone over that a thousand times. Have you bought *their* presents yet, Jason?'

'No, Mother. I'll do it all in one day. I loathe shopping, as you know. I'll do it closer to the time — in a week or so . . . Now, before I go, could you please give Betty a message?'

'Well, you can speak to her if you like.'

'No. Just tell her this,' said Jason with a quick laugh, 'that I'm going to write a book like *Wuthering Heights* — or I'm going to *try* to, at least.'

Jason's mother laughed at this in return; then added 'As if you would want to, Jason': and then with many exchanges of love and affection, their conversation came to an end.

If Hampshire was bright and sunny that day, Cumbria and its Lake District were the opposite; for there it was grey and gloomy, and with a steady drizzle of rain sprinkling down from out of the skies; and which made a fire burning in an open grate all the more cheerful, seen through the windows of Gillian's mother's house, where the curtains had not been drawn, and where the fierce blaze of its flames lit up the deep recess of a fireplace; before which Gillian and her mother were seated as they were inclined to do, once the children had gone to bed — and which, in spite of the differences between them, they enjoyed.

'So, the children are going to London,' stated Gillian's mother.

'Yes, they are,' answered Gillian, 'between Christmas and the New Year.'

'Oh, it's definite is it? I thought —'

'Well, it's as definite as I can expect it to be, Mother. When I've spoken to Jason, I can hear that he would *like* it to happen, but there is always the sense of a question in his mind, as if he can be sure of nothing.'

'Perhaps he doesn't really want to have them,' her mother answered. 'Perhaps it is all a pretence . . . Men can be like that, Gillian. You know that. Say one thing and mean another.'

'And so can women,' answered Gillian sharply. 'It's not only true of men, Mother. Women can be like that as well.'

'Not in *my* experience, Gillian,' answered her mother, with a stern expression on her face.

'Are you speaking of Father, Mother?'

'I am — yes. He wasn't reliable, as you know. Always full of fancy ideas that couldn't be realised.'

'But that was what was delightful about him, Mother: why everyone loved him. How can you criticise him for that?'

'You weren't married to him, Gillian,' was all her mother could voice in reply; as if to imply that she didn't wish to discuss the subject further, and as she fiddled with her beads and looked at the darting flames of the fire, that were reflected in her eyes, and that allowed Gillian to retreat into herself, and to reflect upon what the true cause of her mother's bitterness might be.

'Shall I make us a drink?' Gillian asked.

'What time is it?'

'Well, it's getting on for eleven,' said Gillian, looking at a tall grandfather clock that was ticking away in the background.

'Oh, well – then, yes. A drink would be nice. Horlicks for me, I think. I had cocoa last night, and it didn't agree with me.'

Gillian rose from her seat and went to leave the room, pausing as she did so to look at the gloomy, rain-filled sky beyond its windows.

'We forgot to draw the curtains, Mother,' she said crossing towards the windows to close them.

'I wasn't aware of it,' said her mother, in an abstract manner, as if she hadn't heard what her daughter had said, and with her mind preoccupied by secret thoughts, in which she spent so much of her time.

'Horlicks, you said, Mother?' asked Gillian.

'Yes, dear,' her mother replied. 'I prefer it. It makes me sleep better.'

XVII

ONE WEEK LATER Jason was unwell again, and had still not bought his Christmas presents: and John and Billy, who had done no more as yet than to draw up a list, were quarrelling over theirs.

'Well, do we buy Mr Callow something or not?' asked John.

'I don't know,' said Billy. 'What do you think?'

'I was asking you what *you* thought, Billy. Do you want us to, or not?'

'Yes. Perhaps.'

'Well, *what* then? You can't decide about your own present, so what about his?'

'Well, it looks as if he could do with a scarf. That frayed old thing he wears is disgusting.'

'Right, then – a scarf,' said John, tersely, adding Jason's name and present to their list.

'And when do we do it?' asked Billy.

'Do what? Buy it?'

'Yes – when?'

'Tomorrow,' said John decisively. 'We buy everything tomorrow. We get it done. It's Saturday. We'll get *every*thing. Have it all finished ... Why is it that we always get in such a bloody big mix-up over Christmas?'

'I don't know,' said Billy, 'but we do.'

'And are we going out to eat tonight, or not?' asked John.

'By the look of the weather, we might as well stay in,' said Billy. 'There's fog everywhere. You can't even see across the street.'

'That's settled it then,' said John. 'We stay in, and we buy Mr Callow a scarf tomorrow; and we get all the other presents as well.'

'To show Mr Callow that we like him,' said Billy.

'To show him that we like him,' repeated John.

Billy went into the kitchen to arrange something for supper: then called out, 'Do you know who I saw today, John?'

'Father Christmas.'

'I wish I had. No, it was Darren Fawcett.'

'Oh, *him*. What did he have to say?'

'I bumped into him in Sloane Square. He was just coming out of the tube. Going to the Royal Court, he said, to pick up some tickets.'

'What for?'

'For what's playing there, I suppose. The revue we went to. He's been away – in "rep". In Guildford, I think he said. Playing bit-parts. Making some money for once.'

'Good.'

'You don't like Darren, do you, John?' said Billy.

'No. He's too bloody creepy – slippery's more the word. I'd never trust him over anything.'

'Oh,' said Billy, teasingly, 'how *severe* you are.'

'I feel a *need* to be, with him. I don't think you should be seeing him.'

'I'm not . . . or not very often', was Billy's reply.

'Or think of him as a friend.'

'He's just another actor,' said Billy.

Billy went on with his preparations for supper, and John went into the bathroom to tighten a screw that had become loose beneath one of the bathroom shelves.

'Did you really mean what you said?' asked Billy, coming to join him and to watch what he was doing.

'About what?' asked John.

'About Darren. That he's no good.'

'I did,' said John, firmly. 'I've said it before, and I won't say it again.'

'O.K,' said Billy, accepting his friend's judgement, 'I won't see him.' And with that, he went back to the kitchen.

The fog that had descended upon the city was especially dense that night – partly because of a reliance upon coal-fires for heating in so many of London's houses; and which made the cityscape at that time such a different one from what it is today; with smoke rising from countless chimneys, and with the persistent smell of it in the air.

But unlike John and Billy, Jason had been undaunted by the weather, and had wrapped himself up warmly and gone out. He hadn't quite gone back to his previous habit of wearing two overcoats as well as a scarf and a pair of mittens; but he had put on a particularly heavy, winter coat, that had a large, generous collar, which he had turned up in order to protect his face and his ears. For in those days, the fog could almost sting, and could cause the skin to tingle – which, combined with the cold, could make one feel uncomfortable in the extreme.

Joseph had said that he might meet Jason for a drink at their local pub; but for once hadn't shown up; and Jason had gone on to one of the small restaurants that he frequented in the area, and had indulged in a heavy meal and a decent bottle of wine. But although he felt comforted by this – comforted, that is, from a physical point of view – his mind was troubled. For days now, he had again felt that pull that he would experience at times, and that drew him away from the surface of life:

that peculiar form of listlessness from which he suffered, and that made him so passively inactive and so incapable of asserting himself: not wanting to wash himself or to bathe; not caring about the fact that his body began to smell, and that this transferred itself onto his clothing; particularly onto his underclothes; which he didn't change and in which he slept; and that would almost begin to reek.

The squalor of this he didn't enjoy exactly – that would be a misleading word to use – but he passively accepted it, knowing, at the same time, that the remedy was such a simple one. Just a few, firm decisions that would swiftly return him to the present; the buying of his Christmas presents being one of them.

He didn't read at such moments: didn't even listen to music: just sat in his room, allowing the day to go by: sometimes – less often now – walking the streets alone, and identifying in some way with the collective mass of people that he would pass on the crowded pavements, or with whom he would mingle in the shops. He had had a few reflective thoughts on occasions – but these were extremely limited ones, when one considers what a lot goes on in a person's mind in moments when they do nothing. And these had included thoughts about Arnold; and about John and Billy having discovered him, lifeless upon the carpet.

No affection, no sentiment, had been stirred in him by this. It was simply the hard fact of Arnold's death that filled his mind; combined with the image of Arnold's body, lying with its hairpiece free of its head.

He also had thoughts about his parents and about their age, which he had suddenly become aware of when he had last gone to visit them: particularly that of his father, whose health had recently declined a little. And had there been no fog, clear skies and a moon – then, no doubt, as he made his way home, he would have released one of those disturbing, animal-like moans of his.

But the fog that night was extremely dense – a heavy, cold, almost gruesome one; so that, as he entered a turning off the King's Road that led towards the river, and to the dark, rambling house in which he lived (and which, when he went out, he now thought of as being empty), he looked more like some figure out of the Victorian age, than one of post-war London.

No one passed him as he made his way along; and because of the curtains being so drawn against the weather, there were no lights in the houses that lined the street – where an occasional holly-wreath, that had been placed over a door knocker, seemed dead and ghostly, as if it might be a forgotten wreath placed upon a tomb, rather than the symbol of Yuletide greetings and good cheer for which it was intended.

There was no such wreath, of course, on the door of Jason's house. Nothing was different or seasonal there. Time for Jason stood still; and the approach of Christmas was playing no part in his life. Not even the thought that he would be seeing his children before the New Year. Yet he was acutely conscious of the fact that he was feeling neither sad nor sorry for himself, in the way that he had so often done in the past in such moments of mental crisis. On the contrary, he now felt a kind of hard, fixed calm; as if inside him, buried within him, and deep within the caverns of his mind, he knew that he was at last close to a real encounter with himself, and that the deepest truth of his life – its deepest story – would soon be properly revealed.

The following day, and in an attempt to keep some control of what was happening, Jason made this entry in his notebook.

'Alas, I have slipped back – and I regret it. For a while, things seemed to be moving towards some safer kind of ground, and I had allowed myself to be pleased with that.

'Oh! How stupid can I be? Have I not yet learned that the irrational *is* irrational? That it is precisely at those moments when I begin to think that I shall be well, that the monster comes to claim me? . . . And who – what – *is* this thing that possesses me? That makes me so passive, so inactive? Is it some game played by the gods – some tease – that allows men (and women too, of course) to forget the darkness of their origins and that they are mostly composed of ignorance?

'I have heard all the arguments: that Oedipus did not know it was his mother he had married; that incest was his lot, his destiny; and that he therefore cannot be blamed for it. So why should I think that I can escape this pull towards the dark? Might it not be *my* lot to have steered my boat too much against the tide, and that now, having reached mid-age, my strength fails, as it inevitably must, and the tide begins to draw me in an opposite direction.

'Whatever, one can only *try* to know and to be aware: of oneself: of one's makeup: one's story – one's *proper* story that is. I have done my very best to remember my dreams – knowing, as I do, that that is where one's true story lies; but try as I will, their images will not come to me. I am blocked, it seems, cut off from the rich seam of that world, and therefore cannot call on it for help – which is a sorry, perhaps even tragic, state of affairs.

'The one thing that gives me relief is that I at last no longer feel sad – no longer feel sorry for myself. Slowly, I am coming to an acceptance of a kind, and know that what will be will be. Some people reading this – if such a thing should ever take place – might feel cross, or angry, because of my saying this: might mutter to themselves that "all he needs to do is to make an effort." But isn't writing *this* an effort? Am I not fighting for light – for consciousness – by setting down these thoughts? That certainly is what they are meant to be doing.

'I have said nothing to Joseph about this matter, yet I count him my best friend; and I respect his mind; his occasional flights of sudden insight: his unusual powers of interpretation; of seeing things another way round – and cannot help wondering why this should be. Do I not *want* to share my troubles, except by writing of them here? For now that I come to think of it, I have spoken of them to no one. That could be the writer in me, I suppose, that guards his secrets, and that thinks of everything as material for his egotistical practice: the one of wanting to put words of a kind around every type of experience.

'Whatever, I have tried my best to be honest and to have looked myself square in the face – warts and wrinkles and all (as I think I have said before on some previous page). Morally, people could say, I suppose, that I am weak. But is that true? The largest actions – the ones that govern us, that rule over us, are surely ones that lie outside the moral code: that are impersonal – abstract almost. And is there not something of that that is at work in me, and that I am being forced to recognise and to honour?

'This at least I do know; that whatever my weaknesses may be – and like all humans, I have many – I am not being at all weak in this desire I have to in some way grasp my fate; and to face whatever it is, or whatever it might be, towards which I am being drawn. It may be a dangerous thing to do; but all life – all *real* life – is dangerous. Nothing that is real is safe. It is highly charged, volatile, explosive. The calm I feel begins to tell me this; which may seem a curious thing to say; but not if one thinks of words like "the lull before the storm" – when animals blink their eyes, as if in knowledge of the upheaval yet to come; and knowing, as they appear to do, that its advent is inevitable.

'I think now of my family. Think of my parents – of my wife, my children, my brother – and of *his* wife and children too. Something tells me that at some time in the future they will be reading this; and I therefore need to let them know that they are in my mind; and that if, being truthful, I feel no really deep, no really passionate love for who they are, and for what they represent, I do feel concern. Concern that they will go on; that they will continue; and will live their lives out with some success; and wishing for them, as I am doing now, that their stories will be less painful ones than mine.

'Mother, father – pray for me. Jeremy, by brother – pray for me. Joseph, my friend – pray for me. Betty, John and Billy – all pray for me. And for my wife, Jill, and for Tom and Sarah, my two children.

'I do not know a god. I know only of something more un-named than that; a force, a drive, an energy, that governs us, and to which we must relate. Pray to that, please – all of you; that I may be freed from the horrible tension that I suffer, and so know, at last, at least a little of who I am . . . For who needs more than that?; than to know themselves: to have truly looked at themselves in the mirror, and to have seen there something of who they are?'

'Betty, dear,' said Lilian Callow, and speaking quietly, 'we'd better not wake him, I think. He's slept soundly all afternoon and his colour has now come back. We'll let him sleep on – and dine later; or *I* will; and you, perhaps, will bring something in to him on a tray.'

'Oh, I'll do that gladly, Mrs Callow. It's been such a shock to me, seeing Mr Callow collapsed like that, as if some great scene in some great book I had read had suddenly come true.'

Lilian Callow smiled gently at this remark, knowing that Betty's humour was serving at that moment as a cover for deeper emotions; and because she had seen how disturbed Betty had been when she had found her husband unconscious in his chair.

'I took one look at him,' Betty had said, 'and just knew he wasn't with us, if you know what I mean; and that it wasn't the land of nod he had gone to either; it was somewhere deeper than that.' For which reason a doctor had been called, and Edgar had been placed in a bed that Betty had quickly made up in his study, where he had remained asleep for most of the day.

'Shouldn't you ring Mr Jeremy, at least?' Betty had then asked Lilian, expressing a concern she felt that something more serious might soon happen. 'Not Jason, though,' she added, 'because it could upset him too much. But you should ring Mr Jeremy.'

'I'll do it in the morning, Betty. Don't worry, I won't keep it to myself.'

'Are you *sure*, Mrs C, that you can wait until then?'

'Yes, Betty, I am sure,' answered Lilian, pressing Betty's hand. 'I am *sure* . . . Now; let's leave him, and lay the table for dinner. Even if two places aren't used, one *has* to be. For I must eat.'

The two women went off, half closing the study door

quietly as they left, and both comforted by the fact that their patient had now begun to snore: a snore that grew louder as the evening wore on, so that its sound echoed throughout the ground-floor rooms of the house; and one that provoked a smile on the face of Lilian, and eventually, a gentle chuckle of laughter from Betty.

'I wonder if Jason has bought his presents?' Lilian said to Betty, after she had eaten alone, and after Betty had come into the dining room to help clear away the things.

'It's funny you should say that, Mrs C,' was Betty's reply, 'I was wondering about that this morning as well.'

'I expect that by now he will have,' said Lilian, 'although I've not heard from him for a week, you know; so I am hoping nothing is wrong; and that he's not slipped back again or something.'

'Oh, he's just busy, I expect – that's what it'll be,' said Betty, who, for once, was not using her instinct. 'He hates shopping, as we've all been told goodness knows how many times over the years. So it will have been an effort for him; and he's been made grumpy by it too, I expect,' she added, with a laugh.

'I'm sure you're right,' said Lilian. 'He'll ring tomorrow.'

'Or the day after,' said Betty, still not speaking out of her deepest thoughts.

'Or the day after, then,' repeated Lilian, as she put cutlery into a drawer, and as she turned to listen to the sound of her husband's snore, and to the slow but steady rhythm of his breathing.

XVIII

EDGAR CALLOW WAS not seriously ill. At first, his wife believed that he had suffered a minor stroke; but the doctor was sure it was not the case; and, after sleeping that night until close to ten o'clock, Edgar woke feeling refreshed and almost himself again. And it was exactly at that time that his second son, Jason, who was so loved and admired by his mother, and for whom he had a rather strong affection himself, returned once more to the house in which he lived; and after having been out yet again to dine alone at one of his local restaurants.

That night, the sky was clear, and there was no fog; and the stars winked and twinkled in a blue-black sky; and in a way that made Jason strangely happy. He still felt that threat of a danger within him, and in that sense still felt troubled; but the calm he had been experiencing of late was still at work, and he reminded himself of how pleased he should be to be living in such a well-known part of London: so rich in artistic history, with its memories of Turner and Carlyle; of Whistler and Oscar Wilde.

And now, this night, as he walked home, a strength of will at last came back to him; making him determine that he would return once more to the smaller things of life; to being clean and decently dressed again; with his hair and beard trimmed properly; and to buying the Christmas presents that he had planned to buy – including a pair of braces for his father that he had seen in a shop window in Knightsbridge: that were dark green in colour, with pink-beige leather thongs and two smart gold-coloured clips, and that he felt sure his father would like.

As he drew close to what he still thought of as being Arnold's abode, he noticed that on the knocker of the door across the street — that is, on the door of Lady Cynthia's' house — an enormous holly-wreath had been placed; one that was enlivened by fir cones and mistletoe; and topped by a great bow of golden ribbon; and that spoke to him of the spirit of good cheer that is meant to be a part of Christmastime.

Taking his keys out of his pocket, Jason unlocked the door and let himself in; immediately switching on the lights in the main hallway, as was his habit; then closing and bolting the door behind him. But as he crossed towards the staircase and began the climb to his rooms, he heard a knock on the door that he had just closed. Not a heavy knock: and one that seemed to indicate that the caller had seen him come in, and was expecting him to respond to it quickly. So Jason turned back and recrossed the hallway; then unbolted the door and opened it.

Standing outside was a young man that Jason knew at once was familiar to him; although he couldn't place exactly who he was or where exactly he had seen him.

'Mr Callow?' the young man asked.

'Yes,' said Jason politely, but with reservation.

'You don't remember me,' the young man said.

'I'm afraid I don't,' replied Jason, although the young man's dark, quick-moving eyes were stirring a memory in his mind.

'We met some months ago,' said the young man, 'in a coffee bar: on the King's Road.'

'I don't remember it,' said Jason, and in spite of the fact that the memory of it was now coming back to him.

'I sat down opposite you – at table.'

'Some months ago, you said?' asked Jason, thinking that he should be guarded.

'Yes. In August, I think it was.'

'Oh. Well. Yes. Perhaps I do. Did we speak?'

'No. Not very much.'

'Then how do you know my name?'

'By this,' the young man said, producing an envelope from his pocket. 'You left it on the table; which is how I know both your name and your address.'

Jason took the envelope and looked at it, then saw that it was one containing a bill that had been paid; and that he probably hadn't missed because it was acting only as a receipt.

'Oh,' said Jason, 'thank you.'

'I didn't post it, or put it through your letter box, because I thought it would be nice to meet you again. You are a writer – aren't you? I've read two of your books. I did call here once, but an elderly gentleman answered and told me you weren't at home. Then I was away – and have been ever since: at work: in Guildford. I am an actor.'

'Oh,' replied Jason, not knowing what else to say. 'Well, thank you again.'

'Can I come in?' the young man asked.

'How do you mean?'

'Well – have a drink, perhaps: have a talk . . . As I say, I have read your work. I am an admirer of yours.'

Jason hesitated, not knowing what this odd exchange could mean, and whether he should respond to the request or not.

'I won't stay long,' the young man said, speaking in a very gentle manner, and with a quick, fetching smile, 'but I would like it, if you don't mind.'

'Very well,' said Jason. 'I live at the top of the house,

I'm afraid. But do come up, if you wish to. I only have whisky.'

'Whisky would be fine,' the young man answered.

'Very well,' Jason repeated, pulling the door wide-open and allowing the young man to enter – then closing the door behind him, but this time without bolting it.

'Your name?' asked Jason, thinking he needed to know that.

'Darren,' said the young man.

'A nice name,' said Jason.

'Thank you,' the young man replied.

★

It was now close to eleven o'clock, and from the windows of Lady Cynthia's house, strains of Wagnerian music were drifting into the cold night air; and Lady Cynthia, who was in her bedroom, was preparing to go to bed, whilst her lover, Captain Smythe, was downstairs having a nightcap.

'Frederick,' Lady Cynthia called out, having gone to the head of the staircase, and using her lover's Christian name for once, 'you will check the door – won't you? – before you come up.'

'My dear, of course,' came the emphatic reply, in a sharp, military voice.

'And you will turn off the music, as well.'

'That too, my love,' Captain Smythe replied, as he swiftly refilled his glass.

For a while the two lovers remained silent and apart – Captain Smythe lost in his thoughts and enjoying the quiet drink he was having alone; and Lady Cynthia, who was now glad to be in her bed, going over the events of the day; and thinking to herself that she had good cause to be happy, in that she was far from poor – was reasonably well-off, in fact – had quite a nice house, not a flat, in one of the best parts of the city; and that if her lover, Captain Smythe, wasn't exactly all that she desired (in that she was aware of how he could occasionally be unfaithful to her) he did, nonetheless, have his charms – and, for his age, a considerable amount of vigour.

Eventually, however, the time of their separateness came to an end. For the music ceased, and Captain Smythe, having finished his second nightcap, checked to see that the door of the house had been locked; then switched off the lights in the drawing-room and the hall; and then, with a sudden straightening of the back, and a quick clearing of the throat, he made his way to Lady Cynthia's room: not thinking only of her, alas, but also of a plan he had for the following day; which was to rise early and to be off, in the hope of having lunch and possibly dinner with another lady friend of his who happened to live in Greenwich.

XIX

AS JASON POURED his visitor a generous glass of whisky, and then a similar one for himself, he began to feel a curious sense of excitement; one that he quickly recognised as being connected with danger of some kind; and for a moment he wondered whether he should send the young man away and so be rid of him. Perhaps by saying that his brother was coming to spend the night with him, or that his wife was in town and that she was coming to visit. But no, he said to himself, he should continue with what he was doing – pouring the whisky; add water to it if it was asked for (for which purpose, he then decided, he would use the cold-water tap in the bathroom, because it was closer than the kitchen one) and then just see how it went – this very unexpected encounter with someone he had seen just once before in his life; and who, having called at his door, had asked to come in – *and*, with his having said yes to that, to his finding him here – now – in his rooms, and looking perfectly respectable, he thought, with his slightly wavy, auburnish hair brushed back over his ears; and with the neat, black sweater he was wearing, that was clean, well cut, and in a fine, merino wool.

'Water?' asked Jason, holding up a glass.

'A little,' Darren replied, with yet another of his fetching smiles.

'Oh – well. I'll have to get it from the bathroom tap,

if you don't mind,' said Jason. 'I've no jug; and the bathroom's nearest.'

Darren nodded, as if to say that that would be all right, and Jason went off with their two glasses. Then Darren suddenly called out after him, 'Do you mind if I use your lavatory, Mr Callow?'

Jason came to the door of the bathroom, not having quite heard what Darren had said.

'I beg your pardon?' said Jason. 'The tap . . . I didn't quite hear.'

'Can I use your lavatory, please?'

'Oh, yes . . . yes, of course,' Jason answered, 'It's in here.'

Darren, whose movements were of a highly controlled and graceful kind, crossed the room as Jason returned to it; then went into the bathroom and closed the door. And it was then that, in the chair in which Darren had been sitting, Jason saw a knife – indeed, saw almost a dagger, since its blade was held in a sheath, and it had a large and elaborately moulded handle.

This unexpected sight made Jason curious rather than nervous, however, because his first reaction was to see it more as some piece of stage-property, that might be used in a pantomime, than as any really serious kind of weapon.

'Very theatrical,' were words that came to his mind, and that rather fitted in, he thought, with Darren's personality – or with what he had gathered of it so far.

Placing Darren's glass on a table next to where he had been sitting, Jason then retreated to his chair to await his visitor's return: still very curious about him, and about what might be about to occur. For he had an idea that this meeting held a great meaning for him; almost as if he had known about it beforehand; and he now admitted to himself that when Darren had come to sit opposite him in the coffee bar, some spark of energy had passed between them, making him think that they might have been in search of each other; and which made him now wonder (if he was to be really truthful about it) whether a degree of sexual attraction might not have been involved. Not that he had had many experiences of that kind, as we know. As he had said to Joseph, only one, in fact; and when he was still a youth and when, rather recklessly, as he saw it, he had indulged in a somewhat sadistic physical exchange with a fellow schoolboy after a shower. An experience that he had then blotted from his mind, and which was of a kind that he had not indulged in since.

'Thank you,' said Darren, coming out of the bathroom, and having now removed his sweater and wearing it slung loosely around his shoulders; and looking most striking, Jason thought, in a darkish, snakeskin-patterned shirt that had a slight sheen to it, as if it might be made of silk, or satin.

'Have you been here long?' Darren asked.

'Three years,' Jason replied.

'On your own?'

'Yes. My wife and I are separated.'

'Oh. I'm sorry.'

'Yes. Well. These things happen.'

'I wouldn't know about that – about marriage, I mean.'

'No; of course, you are still very young – aren't you?'

'But I'll *never* know about it,' said Darren.

'Oh', said Jason, 'I'm sorry.'

'No – *please*. Please don't say you are sorry. Because *I'm* not. I'm not the marrying kind you see,' with which, he gave another of his smiles: then asked, 'Is this my glass?'

Jason nodded to indicate that it was; then pointed to the knife. 'And that, I think, is yours as well.'

'Oh, yes – *thank* you,' said Darren, affecting to be

surprised, and picking up the knife as he sat down. 'It's rather beautiful, isn't it?'

'Frankly, no. I don't think so,' answered Jason.

'Oh, but it *is*,' said Darren, softening his voice, and slowly drawing the knife out of its sheath. 'It's really *beau*tiful. I love it . . . Now,' he asked, 'shall I show you how good it is – how it works?' – with which he suddenly turned the knife towards his chest.

'Look!' shouted Jason, rising swiftly to his feet. And at which moment, Darren plunged the knife between his ribs; or he gave the impression of doing it, rather; then let out a squeal of laughter.

'Did that frighten you?' he asked, turning the knife towards Jason and showing that its blade had retracted into its handle, and that the knife was indeed a false one, similar to a kind used for the stage.

Jason looked at the knife; then looked at Darren and found himself floundering; and he had the impression that Darren had cast some kind of spell or web, in which he had become entrapped.

'I – er,' was all he could say.

'Look,' said Darren, aggressively, 'did it *frighten* you? That's what I asked. *Answer* me – will you?'

Jason found himself unable to reply. All he could do was to stare at Darren's image, and to think how strangely beautiful he was; almost unreal; seeing him as some kind of alien being, since there seemed to be lights in his hair, and his quick-moving eyes glistened with a new intensity as they looked rapidly around the room; then found Jason: then, having scanned his body in some detail, coming to rest at last upon Jason's own dark eyes, that were so similar in colour to his own.

'Who *are* you?' asked Jason, his voice a little hoarse.

'Who am I?' replied Darren, who was now standing and looking down at him. 'I don't know,' he said, 'I never do. I *never* know who I am . . . I am an actor,' he said. 'You are forgetting that. I can be anyone – everyone – no one,' – and with that, he laughed gently and retreated to his chair.

Jason sipped his drink and Darren sipped his, and the two of them sat in silence, allowing the atmosphere in the room to settle and to become a little more real. And after a while, Jason asked Darren quietly about his having read some of his books. 'Two, I think you said.'

'One, actually,' said Darren. 'Two was a lie. I didn't like it.'

'Oh – I thought you were an admirer of mine.'

'That was a lie too,' said Darren with a smile. 'I'm sorry.'

'Then perhaps you would tell me *why* you didn't like them – or didn't like *it* rather.'

'It's just not my sort of thing,' said Darren, nonchalantly. 'Too cold: too cerebral.'

'Oh, I see,' said Jason, looking a little glum.

'Does that disappoint you?' asked Darren.

'Yes and no.'

'How do you mean? How can it be both?'

'I don't know,' sighed Jason, taking a deep breath, 'It would be difficult to explain. Perhaps because one likes to be told that one's work is admired, even if one has grown to dislike it oneself.'

'Why – *have* you?' asked Darren, suddenly interested.

'Yes,' said Jason flatly. 'I have.'

'But that's something serious – surely; for a writer to say that. Not that I know much about literature – but surely, to take against your *own* work is – well, unusual.'

'Probably,' said Jason.

'So what are you going to do about it?'

'*Do* about it?' said Jason, rising to his feet. 'I don't know *what* I am going to do about it. Nothing probably – about anything!' – with which he let out one of those disturbing animal-like moans of his, and moved across to a far corner of the room: where he hugged himself and tried to control his emotions.

Darren, however, showed no reaction to this, and appeared to be unaffected by Jason's behaviour – almost as if he had expected it. And after taking another sip from his glass of whisky, he rose from his chair with a quick, darting movement that gave the effect of his having a part to perform in a play, and that he was about to go on stage.

'You *are* in a mess – aren't you?' he said to Jason, whose back was turned towards him.

'*Aren't* you?' he repeated, when Jason failed to answer. 'Separated from your wife . . . Disappointed by your work . . . Do you have children?'

'Yes,' muttered Jason, still with his face towards the wall of the room.

'How many?'

'Two.'

'How old?'

'In their teens.'

'And what do *they* think of all this?'

'Of all *what*?' asked Jason, showing some anger, and turning to face his questioner.

'Of this mess you are in.'

'I am *not* in a mess!' protested Jason.

'Rubbish,' said Darren with a sneer. 'It's written all over you. A broken man, is what *you* are, Mr Callow.'

'How *dare* you!' Jason shouted back at him, feeling a sudden fierce surge of emotion that he found difficult to handle.

'How dare I?' Darren replied, 'Oh, you don't know *me*, Mr Callow. I'll dare anything . . . like –'

'Like what?'

Darren laughed. 'Like saying that you are a coward, for instance.'

Jason stared at Darren dumbfounded, not knowing what to reply.

'Well – *aren't* you?' repeated Darren.

Again, Jason was unable to answer; and Darren laughed at him a second time. 'Of course you are. You are afraid of everything: of yourself especially . . . You are on the run, Mr Callow. That's what I'm here for – to tell you that.'

'Look,' said Jason, suddenly finding his words, 'I think you'd better go.'

'*Why*? Because I've told you the truth? . . . Oh, Mr Callow: I didn't think you'd behave like this, you know . . . When I saw you sitting opposite me, sipping your coffee, I said to myself, now *there's* someone who has looked himself square in the face; as I have done. *That*, I thought, was what was drawing me towards you; and you towards me. But I was wrong it seems – wasn't I? . . . Now,' he said, as he turned swiftly towards his chair to collect his knife, 'flick this at the side – this little lever – and the blade no longer retracts . . . See? Very clever – isn't it? Natty . . . Now, Mr Callow,' he said, in a strangely threatening way, 'would you like to try it, do you think?'

'Put the thing down,' said Jason gruffly, and with some authority.

Darren didn't move.

'Put it *down*, I say!' repeated Jason.

'Really?' said Darren. 'You really want me to?'

'Yes. I do. Put it down, I say!'

For a moment, Darren still didn't respond, then, in an oddly obedient fashion, he turned and walked back to his chair, where he slipped the dagger into its sheath.

'Then I'd better go,' he said. 'I thought –'

'You thought *what*?' asked Jason.

'I thought – oh, I can't tell you what I *thought*, Mr

Callow. All I can say – all I can tell you is – that I'm sorry.'

'Here is your coat,' said Jason, collecting it from a chair at the back of the room, 'and your scarf as well.'

'I had no scarf.'

'Oh, no,' replied Jason, realising it was his own scarf he was handling, 'it's mine. Now – please – just go.'

'Very well,' answered Darren, slipping on his overcoat and pushing his knife into one of its pockets. 'I thought I had a part to play,' he said, looking directly into Jason's eyes. 'That that is what I was here for. A part in your life, I mean; that I had been called upon to perform . . . That is what an actor does, you see – lives for – to play his role – whatever part might be required of him.'

Jason didn't reply to this. Instead, he simply crossed to the door of the room and drew it open. 'I'll see you down,' he said.

'Thank you,' replied Darren politely, as he moved gracefully to join Jason at the door; and then passed him and went down the stairs; and as Jason followed him in silence to the hallway; where Darren waited for Jason to catch up with him and to open the door that led to the street.

'Do we kiss each other goodbye?' asked Darren, mischievously. 'Or shall we just shake hands?'

'Goodbye,' said Jason, stretching out his hand, which Darren caught hold of lightly, then clasped, then stroked, then pressed.

'You are a strong man, Mr Callow,' he said, 'an unusual one. Perhaps I did wrong to call you a coward. Perhaps you are tougher than I think . . . So,' he asked, 'do we meet again, I wonder?'

'I doubt it,' said Jason.

'You mean, you don't *want* us to?'

'That is not what I said,' answered Jason, surprised by

his own words. 'I said that I *doubt* that we shall meet, and that is what I meant.'

'Very well then,' said Darren with a smile, 'we must doubt that we shall see each other again. Which means probably not, I guess . . . Unless,' he added with a light laugh, 'we meet in some other coffee bar.'

'Unless that', answered Jason, firmly. 'Goodnight.'

Darren stepped out into the street, and paused to look back at the stocky figure who stood in the open doorway. Then, flipping up the collar of his overcoat and drawing it closely around his neck, he walked off into the night.

XX

AS JASON RE-CLIMBED the stairs to his rooms, he felt a deep tiredness come over him, as if he had reached the end of some long sea-voyage; and that what he now needed was to fall exhausted upon some beach and there wait for his strength to return. For which reason, on entering his rooms, he went immediately into the bedroom and – without removing even his shoes – flung himself onto his bed.

At first, no thoughts came to him – no reflections upon Darren's visit. Before him, all seemed blank, featureless, with no shape, no division. But slowly an awareness began to grow in him that, whilst coping with Darren, he had used his strength to *avoid* something, more than to encounter it. What, he did not know. What had been the purpose, had been the meaning, of Darren's elusive exchange; of its suggestive threats; of its innuendoes? And why the knife? For what reason had Darren produced it; then played with it; then turned it from a toy into a weapon that could kill – if that had been what its handler required? Did Darren know something that he didn't know – about himself? He had seen how intuitive Darren was; how he had followed his feelings carefully; testing each moment of their exchange in order to find out where it was meant to go or was meant to lead. And it had led to what? – to nothing: except Darren's acknowledgement as he left that

Jason might not be the coward he had assumed him to be. But what, Jason kept asking himself, had it all meant? – that Darren thought he *needed* the knife? – to use it? – in order to do what? – to kill? Or – this was the question that finally came to him – perhaps to kill himself?

The darkness of these thoughts exhausted Jason even more; and, unable to persist with them further, he turned onto his side and fell asleep; dropping swiftly into his dreams; and into a sleep from which he did not wake until the morning.

XXI

'JOHN. MOVE OVER – will you?'

'Mmm?'

'Move over – *please*. You're always pushing me out of bed.'

'I am not.'

'Yes, you are.'

'There – is *that* better? . . . come here now . . . No – closer . . . Now, is that what you want?'

Billy and John were going through their ritual banter concerning the sharing of their bed, knowing that it would usually end with their making love, and finding it an attractive means of relating.

'Do you think Mr Callow will like the scarf we bought him?' asked Billy, as he snuggled up close to his partner, feeling happy and secure.

'I expect so,' answered John.

'You really think so, John?'

'Yes. Of course I do. We chose it well. It will suit him. It will suit his colouring.'

'I suppose it will.'

'Say, you *know* it will,' said John. 'You're so bloody uncertain about things.'

'I know it will,' Billy answered, obediently.

'I love you,' said John.

'And I love you,' said Billy.

But if John and Billy's night was one of pleasure, the opposite was the case in the house of Jason's parents; for much to everyone's surprise, his father suffered a relapse, and a doctor had to be called during the night. The morning found some improvement, however, and it seemed that the crisis had quickly passed.

'Edgar,' Lilian said to her husband quietly, as he lay next to her, and as the first glimmer of daylight showed beneath the hems of the bedroom's closely-drawn curtains.

'Yes, dear?' Edgar replied.

'How are you feeling? Better?'

'Oh, much. A lot. I've slept. And sleep always does the trick – doesn't it?'

'Yes. It's a great healer. Do you need anything? A hot drink? Some water?'

'No, dear. I don't think so. I am very comfortable – here, with you . . . Did Jason call last night?'

'No, I'm afraid not. He didn't.'

'So we still haven't heard from him.'

'No.'

'And it's almost Christmas.'

'And it's almost Christmas – yes. But he'll ring *today*, I am sure. If not, I'll ring him.'

'Yes, of course. I doubt that there is anything to worry about, Lilian. No news is good news, as they say.'

'Yes. That is the saying – isn't it?' replied Lilian, as she climbed out of bed to slip on a warm dressing-gown; then crossed the room to draw back the curtains, and to reveal a clear, pale winter sky, with the sun just rising above the bare trees of the orchard . . . "Bare trees that glitter near the sky," she said to her husband. 'Do you remember them, Edgar – those words: a poem we used to recite? . . . "The sea's first miracle of blue – bare trees that glitter near the sky?"

'Oh – yes. I do. How lovely.'

'Beautiful – yes,' said Lilian, peering out of the window, '– and our robin is there, you know. Always hopeful. Always cheerful.'

'Which is what *we* must be,' said Edgar.

'Which is what we must be,' responded Lilian, as she drew her dressing-gown around her and returned to her husband's side.

*

'It's quite a nice morning, Mother,' said Gillian, as she brought her mother's breakfast into her bedroom on a tray.

'Is it?' asked her mother, showing no real interest.

'Yes. There is even some sun . . . Look. You can see it reflected in the lake.'

'I can't from here,' her mother replied. 'I can never see the water from my bed.'

'Oh, what a pity. It's really beautiful. Somehow I think that the countryside is at its best in winter – don't you?'

'Not if there's ice and snow,' said Gillian's mother.

'Well, there's none of that, this morning,' said Gillian. 'It's almost springlike.'

'Spring is a long way off, Gillian. You shouldn't be thinking of it – and I hate the winter, as you know.'

'I can't think why, Mother. The house is warm. You are very comfortable here. The walls are solid.'

'Yes, well. We built them – didn't we? Your father and myself. Made them purposefully thick against the weather.'

'And very sensible too,' said Gillian, knowing that she would win no positive response from her mother that morning. 'Yes,' she repeated, 'very sensible,' as she picked up a pair of her mother's stockings. 'Do these need washing?' she asked.

'Oh – yes,' her mother replied, glancing at her daughter in a sly manner, in order to avoid thanking her for her help in such things.

'Well, I'll get it done then. I'll put them in with the children's things: none of which need boiling.'

Her mother said no more. She simply picked up a newspaper that Gillian had brought in to her on the tray and poured herself a cup of tea. And as she flicked through the pages of the paper, and as she took a first careful sip from her breakfast-cup, her daughter wagged her head in an expression of exasperation, then walked out of the room.

In London, in Chelsea, the morning was even brighter than in the country – than in either Hampshire or the Lake District, and Lady Cynthia, who disliked sleeping with her bedroom curtains fully closed, woke to a shaft of sunlight falling upon the head of her sleeping lover; who always looked so vulnerable, she thought, when beside her and asleep; and quite the opposite of the sharp, defensive man that he appeared as during the daytime.

'Fred-er-ick,' she cooed to him softly, knowing that he liked to be wakened gradually.

'Fred-er-ick,' she repeated, blowing gently into his hair and one of his ears, 'it's seven-thirty, you know; and you said you needed to be off early.'

'I what?' Captain Smythe answered, only half awake.

'You said you wanted to get away early, my love, and it's already half past seven.'

'Oh! My God – yes,' he said, now turning onto his back, and as his plans for the day found their way into his mind.

'Well – shouldn't you get up?' said Lady Cynthia, kissing him lightly upon the nose, 'and shave before breakfast?'

'Not just yet,' her lover replied with a grin; his teeth,

yellowed by smoking, showing beneath the bristles of his moustache; '– just one more cuddle – eh? A little romp before I go?' To which request Lady Cynthia graciously gave in, happy, as she always was, to be playful in her lover's arms; and thankful that the day could begin in such a manner, before they had breakfast, and before the inevitable farewells from her bedroom window as she saw the Captain off in his car.

Jason's sleep had been untroubled and unbroken; and he awoke to the day feeling refreshed; his mind quickly filling with memories of the previous night, and of Darren's unexpected visit.

He was still fully dressed, and felt a need to go quickly to the bathroom, where, as he swilled his face, he caught sight of himself in the mirror.

Was he a coward? he asked himself. Was there some truth in that? He stared deeply into his reflected eyes to find that they stared back at him with an untrembling calm. Was he still frightened? Still running away from himself? Still burying his head in sand?

He could hardly think so, for now he felt so sure that he knew himself better than he had ever done: that, even though the entries in his notebook had as yet been few, they had given him a new view of himself – an honest view: that he had at last approached something of a truth about himself: that his story – his 'real' story, as he thought of it – was an odd and unconventional one; and of a man of some intelligence who had been travelling on the wrong train, and along what had always been the wrong track.

The winter sun was sending silver-gilt beams of light into his rooms; and as he returned to his bedroom, he crossed to its window to look down at the garden below.

It was as shapeless and disordered as ever. Nothing had changed. The broken urn still lay across one of its pathways.

The weeds, now lessened by winter, still pushed their way between the cracks in the garden's paths; and the now leafless briars and brambles still spilled unchecked across the tops of the garden's walls – beyond which, looking towards the south, he could see the embankment and the river, which, with the tide being high, stretched in a level grey towards Battersea, where a set of barges tethered together made their slow progress upstream; and where a police-boat swiftly passed them, its lights still on, in spite of the sun being up, and with its small white prow sending quick wavelike movements towards the shore.

On the opposite side of the river, a man was walking a dog; his steady rhythm showing that it was something he did each day and probably at the same time; and Jason wondered how long it might be that he had followed this routine. For how many years? – and for how long might he go on following it in the future?

Life goes on, he thought; is still going on; will go on going on – for each of us, until the end.

'There's one funeral you're sure to be at,' he heard Betty's voice say, as he had heard it said so may times, 'and that's your own'; at which he smiled, thinking to himself how fond of her he was, and of how, in a way, she had been a kind of mother to him. A very different one to his real mother – to Lilian: for Betty had provided him with a certain weight, a certain earthiness, that his own mother had lacked, and he felt glad of it.

Turning from the window, Jason moved to the chest at the foot of his bed, where the one notebook he had used lay open; and picking it up, he fingered through its pages, reminding himself of the things that he had said in it. Then, quite irrationally, he decided that he would open the chest, and that he would then hide the notebook beneath whatever there might be stored in it: which he quickly did. Then he closed the chest and turned its key in its lock; then withdrew the key and crossed to slip it into a small, china vase that stood on a shelf close to his alarm clock.

Having done that, he found that he then entered an almost trance-like state of mind, and realised that he was looking at the various objects in the room – a chair, his bed, his shirts, his articles of underwear that were strewn here and there – with a curious objectivity. All seemed to be defined with a hard, cold clarity; as if each of them had been drawn by a firm hand upon thickish sheets of paper, and as if he was noting and recording it in detail.

From his bedroom he passed into the living room where Darren had sat the previous night, and where, in his imagination, he could see with equal clarity the dagger Darren had produced, and of which he had claimed to be fond.

He saw Darren handling it; heard his voice: reminded himself of how unreal it had all seemed at the time, and thought how unreal it still seemed now.

Then he saw Darren at the door as he left, felt the pressure of his hand upon his own; pressing it, stroking it. And then the final image of Darren, with his coat collar turned up and drawing it closely around his neck as he went walking off into the night.

Now, he no longer pondered upon the meaning of Darren's visit. He accepted it as having been a part of his life; as being something that had happened to him, and that had been meant to happen – as we are obliged to do with all experience.

By this time, Lady Cynthia and Captain Smythe had finished their breakfast, which Lady Cynthia always insisted that they have in bed upon a large, silver tray; and which she partly enjoyed because she could then linger on and watch her lover as he dressed – admiring the smart, military fashion in which he would slip his braces over his shoulders, having first stuffed his shirt-tails into his trousers; and then, leaning forward slightly, how he would do up, with equal precision, the buttons of his flies – and then, in one swift movement, pass a hand across his moustache.

'Frederick,' she said, as he slipped on a boldly checked waistcoat, and then did up the buttons of that, 'I do love you, you know.'

'And I do you, my dear,' he answered, without turning to look at her, 'my God I do.'

'Well – shall I see you tomorrow?' she asked.

'Tomorrow?' he replied, 'Yes, perhaps. I'm not sure. I'll ring. But the day after, certainly . . . Now,' he added, 'I must be off. Duty calls . . . I've my mind upon a car I've seen in Greenwich – a real beauty: and you know how I am, once I am set upon such things.'

'Of course, dear,' Lady Cynthia answered generously. 'You and your *cars*'; with which she let out an engaging ripple of laughter, that seemed full of light and sunshine; as was her room, with the large bowlful of roses that Captain Smythe had brought her the day before, standing upon her dressing-table; surrounded by her assortment of silver-backed hairbrushes, together with the framed photograph of her late husband that appeared to preside over the room.

'Well, I'll see you off from the window,' said Lady Cynthia, 'as usual.'

'As you always do,' said Captain Smythe, with a sudden look of real affection, and crossing to Lady Cynthia's side of the bed to give her a farewell kiss.

'And you *will* ring,' said Lady Cynthia.

'I'll ring,' he answered. 'I can't say quite when – but I'll ring.'

Unaware that his mental rhythms has begun to accelerate, Jason was now moving swiftly from room to room;

inspecting each of them carefully; and seeming to fix them even more permanently in his mind. Then, all of a sudden he collapsed into a chair and wept. Not because he was feeling sorry for himself, but because the tension in him had broken and had given him a feeling of release.

The relaxation provided by this brought many reflections into is mind. He saw quick pictures of his childhood; of himself playing with Jeremy by the river beyond the orchard of his parent's house in Hampshire. He saw pictures of his first meeting with Jill, which had been a chance one, when they were both extremely young; neither of them realising that they were later to re-meet and become drawn to each other. He saw his children, Tom and Sarah, when they were small, and remembered how attractive they had been and were still. He saw Betty's plump figure, stooping in the kitchen to store away the various pots of jam that she would make each year, having labelled each with sticky labels, and having covered their tops with a circle of greaseproof paper and then a larger one in linen. He saw his friend, Joseph, when he too was young, and they had first met and argued in a bar on the Fulham Road; and recalled how bright and alive he had appeared to be; remembering his curiosity of mind, the vibrancy of his physical energy and presence. He also remembered Arnold, and how strange he had seemed, when he had first gone to rent the suite of rooms in which he had lived for the past three years. He saw John and Billy on the stairs before they came to know him, in their neat suits and their neatly knotted ties, and the way in which they would lower their eyes whenever he passed, and would murmur 'good evening' or 'goodnight'. He saw his father and mother, not as they were then, but as they had been some twenty years previously: saw his father's bespectacled eyes, always peering, always questioning: saw his slightly stooping, wiry frame: saw his mother's fine, near-classical features, with her hair already drawn back into a bun, and her gentle, understanding smile, that expressed the reasonableness of her nature. He saw so many things of the past: so many images of people, places, things – memories of which came flooding back to him; until, eventually, his weeping ceased – and, feeling tired by the release that he had been given, he decided to lie down again upon his bed: which he then did; still with his shoes on, and lying stretched out upon his back, and with his hands clasped behind his head.

And it was then that the sense of some great action came to him; the feeling that something was about to take hold of him and drive him to do he knew not what. How it came to him he couldn't tell, but the sense of it happening was clear and sure and firm in his mind and his intelligence rose to meet it; so that he no longer felt nervous and afraid, in the way that he had so often done when he had had similar experiences in the past. The fight had at last gone out of him. He felt almost a sense of grandeur about the moment; as if his story – the one that he had so ardently been seeking – was about to arrive at its conclusion. Indeed, he experienced something close to joy, a kind of happiness: a sense of order and rightness. 'Thy will be done,' were words that came to him; and something Joseph would often say when speaking about the *I Ching* – words in which he so delighted – 'Fate comes when it will and thus we are ready.'

For a while, Jason remained on his bed without moving; during which time the sunshine had increased in strength and had filled his rooms with a great flood of light. He could hear birds singing in the garden, glad that the winter should have withdrawn its icy fingers, and that there was no threat of frost or snow that might deprive them of their nourishment.

From the river, he could hear the faint sound of a tug

chugging away, the low throb of its engine just reaching him, setting a steady rhythm in his mind, and reminding him that the life of the city was continuing. Soon, he thought, he would hear noises in the street; of milk being delivered, perhaps – which were sounds with which he was familiar – and it suddenly occurred to him that he too must be up and be going, in much the same way that a man rises from his bed and hurries off to work. 'Ah – well,' he muttered to himself, 'what will be will be' – words that helped to define what he was feeling, and that served, at the same time, as some kind of protection against it as well. And with that, he got up from his bed; quickly found his overcoat (which, as he quite often did, he had thrown across his bed, rather than hang in one of his cupboards) and, putting it on, decided to go and take what he thought of as one last look at himself. 'Before what?' he asked. 'Before I go,' his mind replied, and seeming to provide him with an answer.

In the mirror, he saw his face yet again, now unmarked by trouble and free, it appeared, of all care – and he smiled at himself and flicked his fingers at his image; his dark eyes looking back at him without movement.

Then, at last, the action took hold of him, and submitting to it willingly, he strode out of the room.

Once he had reached the hallway at the foot of the staircase, Jason paused and stood still; his eyes concentrating upon the bolted door ahead of him. Then he crossed to unbolt the door and to open it.

The street outside was empty and the early morning sunshine was falling upon the row of houses that stood facing him – where, looking up, he saw the veiled figure of Lady Cynthia behind the gauze of her bedroom curtains, waiting to wave goodbye to her lover as he sped past on the way to Greenwich. And as Jason saw her, she saw him

– and retreated a little; perhaps because she was made shy by being seen and because of what she was doing.

And it was then that Jason heard and recognised the sound of Captain Smythe's car, that had been parked in a street nearby. He knew the sound of it well; knew it was the Captain leaving early; and he knew as well that in a second or two the car would turn the corner and pass in front of his door: and – because he had seen it arrive and depart so often – he also knew that it would be travelling at quite a speed.

And it was as that last thought came into his mind, that he knew the moment for which he had been seeking had arrived; that he had at last been given the chance to free himself from all the tension he had suffered and so bring his story to an end.

This knowledge came to him in one swift movement; telling him – urging him – to do what he must do. And it was as he thought that thought, that he stepped out of the house and onto the pavement; and then, as the Captain's car sped around the corner, and as the roar of its engine throbbed in Jason's ears, making him think that he was about to encounter some wild animal that had been stalking him for years, Jason threw himself recklessly into the roadway; was struck by the car; was thrown headlong against the pavement's edge; which cracked open his skull, killing him instantly.

PART FIVE

XXII

THE CORONER'S INQUEST that would look into the cause
of Jason's death took place on a bitter January morning at
a magistrate's court in Westminster; and since she was the
only person to have seen how the death occurred, the sole
witness to be called was Lady Cynthia Barron. For she had
watched the event in horror; seeing Jason literally throw
himself in front of her lover's car; seeing him collide with
it; and then be thrown against the pavement's edge and
be killed.

That is what she would tell the coroner and the jury:
and she would say to them as well that she had no doubt
in her mind that Jason had acted deliberately: that he had
appeared consciously to wait for the Captain's car to turn
the corner and had used it to take his own life.

What she would also say she had witnessed was how her
lover had quickly slammed on the car's brakes, creating
an enormous screech — and how, in an attempt to avoid
a collision, Captain Smythe himself had been injured, in
that he had been thrown through the car's windscreen:
and that this had resulted in his having a badly bruised
and battered head and a number of his ribs being broken
— from which, alas, he had not yet fully recovered.

The courtroom was a slightly dismal place, not very warm
and not very well lit, so the jurors were wrapped in their

winter overcoats, their pale, nervous hands (for none of them had served on a jury before) showing that the experience was making them nervous.

At the front and to one side of the courtroom sat Lady Cynthia; and next to her sat Jason's brother, Jeremy, and his wife, Helen (Jason's parents being too shocked and upset to attend). Then, towards the back of the court, sat Jason's friend, Joseph, looking disturbed and deeply unsettled, and wearing a shirt and tie for once, which changed his appearance considerably, and made him seem to join company with John and Billy, who were seated immediately behind him, and who, as usual, were also wearing shirts and ties beneath their neatly buttoned-up overcoats.

Jill — Jason's wife — sat alone, to the left, on the opposite side of the court. She had spoken to Jeremy and his wife (neither of whom she had seen for quite some time) and had explained that she would prefer to be sitting alone because she had such complex emotions to cope with.

The three of them had met earlier for a brief talk, and had shared ideas concerning Jason's mental condition: all of them saying that, aware though they had been that Jason had been acting strangely in recent months, none of them had realised how serious it was (any more than had Betty or John and Billy, or Joseph or Jason's parents).

Unfortunately, it wasn't until a few weeks later that Jason's notebook was discovered, and that would have provided the court with a more clearly defined picture of Jason's state of mind; which meant that it was only through information provided by Jason's parents that the coroner had an indication of how unwell Jason had been. As a result of this, the coroner had pointed out, it would be the evidence of Lady Cynthia that the jury would need to lean upon in order to arrive at their decision — and, being the only witness to be called, and having sat on so many charity commissions and the like, Lady Cynthia was conscious of her position as far as the court hearing was concerned. For which reason, she had dressed herself in an imposing manner, wearing a long mink coat over a fine, pale blue jersey suit; with long, champagne-coloured gloves, ruffled beneath her coat sleeves; and with two enormous strings of pearls falling over her breast and mingling with the silky hairs of her coat; and wearing one of her large, floppy blue hats – one with a particularly large brim – that set off the golds of her hair and the heavy pinks of her complexion.

The coroner had taken his place at a desk close to the jury; who were at his left; with the witness stand in front of them; and he had already gone through all the various details that had been provided to him by the police and by Jason's parents, as well as by Captain Smythe, who had been visited in hospital. Also, he had already suggested to the jurors that rather than a straightforward road accident, this appeared to be a case of a rather unusual form of suicide.

However, he had pointed out to them that the evidence they would need to consider most carefully would be that given by Lady Barron. For although there was enough suggestive evidence to support the idea that the deceased, Mr Callow, had been suffering a depression of some kind, it was insufficient to prove that the depression had been so severe as to speak of Jason as having been seriously unbalanced. And Lady Barron, he pointed out, was the only person to have actually witnessed the moment of death. Other neighbours, he had added, had quickly rushed to the scene: had comforted Lady Barron, and had called the police and an ambulance; but they had all arrived only after the event, and therefore had no evidence to offer.

The coroner was a tall, big-boned man in his early forties – quite good-looking, if in a somewhat boyish way, with his short, blond hair brushed neatly to one side; and he had all the markings of having attended a public school, in the sense that he obviously had a very disciplined and orderly mind, but less control over his body – a difference of which he was only partially aware.

As soon as he had completed his talk, the coroner called upon Lady Cynthia to give evidence; and after making something of a fuss with her coat and her pearls (making sure that the coat was pushed more widely open and that the pearls were more properly displayed) she made her way to the witness-box in a surprisingly quick series of steps, as if she was launching herself towards it. But then, once there, she drew herself up to her full height, placed her gloved hands upon the front of the stand, and showed that she was now prepared to answer any questions that might be put to her.

Before doing this, however, she had made sure that she had caught the coroner's eye. Only briefly (she knew that it must be no more than that) but enough, at least, to have established some kind of personal contact. It wasn't a flirt, exactly, but the coroner had quickly shifted his eyes away from her look as a slight blush passed over his face; which Lady Cynthia duly noted, and about which she immediately felt pleased.

'Lady Barron,' said the coroner, now almost staring her in the eye, and speaking in a very formal and impersonal way, 'May I say how very much your being here is appreciated. You must have suffered an enormous shock, witnessing such an event – what happened both to Mr Callow, as well as to your friend, Captain Smythe.'

'Well – it was rather unsettling – yes,' Lady Cynthia replied; 'and it still is, you know. These things take time to get over.'

'Of course they do,' replied the coroner, 'and I therefore regret the fact that I am obliged to ask you to recall what happened in some detail, if you can.'

'I shall do my best,' said Lady Cynthia, with just the hint of a smile, and looking at the jury, and thinking to herself how terribly pale and nervous they all looked, and assuming that they, unlike herself, were obviously unused to public functions of this kind.

'Then perhaps you can relate to us what you saw,' said the coroner. 'We have heard Captain Smythe's statement of what he has been able to remember – which unfortunately isn't a great deal, since he himself was injured.'

'That is correct,' said Lady Cynthia, pushing out her bosom, and seeming to take charge of things. 'He is still in hospital, as you know – now on the way to recovering I am glad to say; but it is true that he can remember little of what happened.'

'But you can,' the coroner almost interjected.

'Yes. I can. I saw it all, alas.'

'From your bedroom window, I understand.'

'Yes. I happened to be there, you see, waiting to say goodbye to Captain Smythe, who had spent the night at my house. And it was early and I hadn't yet dressed, and so was unable to go down to say my goodbyes to him at the door.'

'I understand,' said the coroner, tactfully, admiring Lady Cynthia's openness and honesty, since she had made it obvious by what she had said, and also by the way in which she had said it, what type of relationship it was that she and the Captain enjoyed.

'And you saw Mr Callow open the door of the house, then step out onto its doorstep?'

'Yes. I did. It was a beautiful morning. Lots of lovely sunshine, you know; and I was glad to be standing there at my window. But –'

'Yes, Lady Barron?'

'Well – when Mr?'

'Mr Callow.'

217

'Yes – when Mr Callow opened the door, I took him in at once: and I rather think that he took me in as well. Not that we really knew each other, you see, in that we had never even spoken to each other: but he had become something of a sight, if you like, in the neighbourhood: due to his dress, you know – to what he would wear.'

'Can you explain that to us, perhaps?'

'Well. He had taken to wearing such a lot of clothes – two topcoats at one moment, for example – and had allowed his beard and hair to become unruly – wild-looking, I would say – which made him noticeable. At one time, he had taken to wearing a pair of winter mittens, as well, although the weather was still quite mild.'

'And that is as you saw him that morning?'

'Oh, no! No. He had improved. There had been a distinct improvement. In fact he was looking more neat and orderly than I had seen him for some time.'

'But he was acting strangely, would you say?'

'Well, not strangely exactly. I wouldn't say that. On the contrary, he appeared remarkably calm, as if he was waiting for something that he knew was about to happen. I don't know how else I might describe it.'

'And then?'

'Well, he just stepped out of the door onto the pavement and stood still. Then, as Captain Smythe's car appeared, he literally *threw* himself in front of it. For that *is* what he did – literally *threw* himself at the car – and, as we know, was dashed to death against the pavement's edge.'

'The death, as you are aware, Lady Barron, was due to Mr Callow's skull being cracked open. Did you witness that?'

'Yes – alas – I did; and almost fainted. It was such a very ugly sight – so horrific, you know – and of a kind one doesn't see very often, of course; but I did realise what had happened – yes – and guessed that it must be fatal.'

'So you would say then that the death was a purposeful one. That Mr Callow killed himself?'

'Yes. I would. I have no doubt that his movements were intentional ones. He didn't slip, I mean, or anything like that. No, he stepped purposefully in front of the car, knowing, it seemed, what would happen – or what *might* happen, at least: that he could be killed, I mean.'

'Thank you, Lady Barron. You have been most clear in all you have said, and I apologise again for having asked you to go over the scene in your mind. Would you say that Captain Smythe did all that he could to avoid the collision?'

'Oh, definitely. Yes. I have no doubt about that. He braked immediately. The sound of it was quite horrendous; and drowned the sound of the collision itself – of Mr – em – Callow being struck.'

'So you would say that Captain Smythe could in no way be said to be responsible for what happened?'

'No. Definitely not. He is an exceptionally skilled driver – an expert one, I would say; but this was a case in which whatever skills he had were of no use. He had braked at once, as I have said, and there was no way that he could have avoided the collision.'

'Thank you again, Lady Barron; and I would ask you to please thank Captain Smythe for being so co-operative, in providing the court with a statement. He says exactly what you have said; and it would therefore appear to be the case that this was not an accidental death. The jury must decide, of course,' he added, looking towards the set of jurors, and exuding an air of steady authority.

'Well, I do understand that,' said Lady Cynthia, robbing him of that authority with a few words, and once again catching his eye and making him blush a second time; and feeling that she had achieved a kind of conquest. For she had been looking at him occasionally and weighing him up; wondering whether he might be someone nice to have beside her in bed; and whether he was of a type, perhaps, that she would enjoy more than her present lover. That is, until she recalled the dashing character of her Captain's military charms, and pictured him stepping into his trousers and slipping his braces over his shoulders.

'Thank you, Lady Barron,' the coroner said graciously, 'I think that is all we need to hear: and may I repeat once again that your giving evidence here has been appreciated. Perhaps you would care to step down and return to your seat; and I shall ask the jury to adjourn, and then await their decision.'

Lady Cynthia was wise enough not to reply to this, and to leave the control of the proceedings in the coroner's hands; for she was very much on the side of public authority, and saw herself as a pillar of the community: a role that she enjoyed, and one that she always fulfilled with pride.

The verdict was the expected one: that Jason had purpose-fully thrown himself in front of Captain Smythe's car; that his death was therefore not accidental; and that the Captain was free of blame. All of which pleased Lady Cynthia; and which – although they were deeply concerned about the fact that they had not foreseen that Jason would take his life, was accepted by Jason's family and his friends.

The person to be the most affected was Jason's wife. For her, the dark shadow of Jason's story had a deeply disturbing effect upon her mind, and seemed to haunt her; realising, as she did, that she had never really known her husband: that there must have been some entire part of his being of which she was unaware, and that it had gradually come between them.

The vagueness of it troubled her; and she was given no help with this by her mother – who, whenever she found her daughter feeling anxious or depressed, could only say to her that she should never have married such a man. Behind which lay the inference, of course, that no man is reliable; and that all women would be better off without them.

But then in time, Jason's notebook was discovered, hidden in the chest at the foot of his bed. His brother, Jeremy (who was arranging for the furniture to be removed) came across it by chance, tucked between a blanket and a few sheets; and he had immediately rung Jill to tell her of it.

'I think you should have it, Jill,' he had said. 'It will explain so much.' Which it did to her; and which it also did to Jason's parents; as well as to Joseph, who was told about it by Jeremy, and from whom, as we know, Jason had kept his illness a secret.

As for Betty, she was in certain ways the one who was the least able to accept the harsh fact of Jason's death. No story, in *her* mind, should end like this – no story that *she* might ever write, that is. Hers, she imagined, would all have happy endings – and this in spite of the fact that so many of the 'classics' she had read had endings of a quite different kind. And what disturbed her so much was that she had at times ignored her instinct concerning Jason and his behaviour, and so had not acted quickly upon it, as she now believed that she ought to have done.

'Betty, dear; you shouldn't worry about it so,' Lilian had said to her one day. 'There's nothing we could have done. Jason didn't *want* to share it with us – and we have to accept that.'

'Yes, I know, Mrs C,' Betty had replied, 'but sometimes you know things and don't quite know how you know them – don't you? And perhaps one of us should have *made* him talk.'

Lilian hadn't answered this. She saw how determined Betty was to bear guilt: that it was something she felt a need of, though she felt no need of it herself. For to her – to Lilian – if she examined herself closely, she had known for several years that her son's life had been only partly lived: that, good though he had been to her in so many ways, in meeting her desires for him as a son – and, to an extent, in fulfilling all the hopes that she had formed for him – her innate honesty told her that the structure of Jason's life had been a faulty one: the first signs of it showing in the indifference he had begun to show towards his children and his wife: the inexplicable coldness he developed. And then, later, the changes in his appearance: the shadow cast by his physical presence: the troubled look in his eyes. And she was intelligent enough to be sure that Jason trusted her, and that, had he wished to do so, he would have shared his troubles with her: that there was no barrier between them of that kind, and that his affection for both herself and his father was a real one; as, indeed, the entries in his notebook would reveal.

What no one knew about, of course, was Darren Fawcett's night-time visit; and that, none of them would ever know: not even John and Billy. For in obedience to his friend's demands, Billy stopped seeing Darren after the brief quarrel they had over him; and in any case, Darren himself, who had read of Jason's death in the newspapers – where, in one of them, an obituary spoke of 'this distinguished writer of cool, orderly prose, who had less to say perhaps than had been imagined' – though shaken by the news, never divulged his visit to anyone.

Six months after Jason's death, Arnold's house was sold, and builders and decorators moved in to prepare it for its new owners, who were combining Arnold's first floor apartment with the suite of rooms above. And it was on one particularly bright summer's day that one of the builders who were at work on the house, and who was lifting a ladder from a lorry that was parked outside in the street, noticed a dull, red stain on the pavement's edge.

'Looks as if someone dropped a bloody paint-pot there,' he said to a colleague of his with a laugh; not knowing that the stain was one of blood. For the mark of Jason's death was still quite strong, and it would be several months yet again before the autumn's rains would diminish it; and later still before the winter's snows would eradicate it entirely.

EPILOGUE

AT THE BEGINNING of this book, when Jason purchased his new notebooks, he had obviously acted on impulse, and he had bought two books rather than one, because he had sensed, as he himself put it (for it had been more a feeling than an idea) that whatever thoughts he needed to set down in them would become a writing of some length.

Due to his death, however, this proved not to be the case, and one could say that there his instinct had misguided him and its judgement been incorrect.

If there is any moral in this tale, it could therefore be the rather simple one that no one can foretell what the story of their life will be, or how and when it will end. Being wedded to our ignorance, we are blind creatures in that respect, and such knowledge is kept hidden.

One can fairly assume, however, that except for Arnold, who had died earlier, the other characters in this book continued to live on. For how long, none of them could tell. But certainly all of them, in their different ways, would have been affected by what happened. One can imagine how Joseph, for example, would have missed the good company of his friend, and finding himself alone of an evening in some bar, would have rued the loss of a companion with whom he had shared so many ideas. And one can picture this as having had a sobering effect upon his character, and that the exuberance of his intellect might have been curbed by it, as a result.

As for Jason's parents, being no longer young, it is likely that they would have been damaged and deeply shaken by the loss of their second son: but with age comes wisdom, and due to the intelligence of their characters, one can think that they would have worked patiently with their grief, and with time come to make peace with it.

Regarding Betty, it is possible that she would have been frightened by the anger she felt at being forced to confront the reality of such an unhappy end; but no doubt her cheerfulness and humour would have quickly come to her aid; or if not that, then she would have found solace in her books.

John and Billy perhaps would have said little about what had happened, except that it was a dreadful thing that Jason had done. But at night, when they were in bed, one can think that they might have recalled, in a reflective manner, the slight but unusual friendship they had shared with Jason for a while – to which Billy might have added as relief, 'But he was in a mess, John. He couldn't even boil a bloody egg.'

As for Jason's wife, Jill, one can guess how badly scarred her mind must have been by the savagery of Jason's end; and for years afterwards, might have found fault with herself for not having seen in time that Jason was so ill; believing, as people are inclined to do, in their capacity to save others. But because her nature was an honest one, one can think that eventually she would have freed herself from guilt; and that she would have come to understand that what had arisen between her and her husband, and that had driven them apart, was something of too large a kind with which to wrestle, and that what her duty now had to be was to attempt to forge a new life for herself: to remarry, perhaps; to learn to be even more patient with her mother; and to love and care for her children.

As for them – for Tom and Sarah – one can picture how hurt they must have been when they had been told the awful news that their father had taken his life; but fortunately, the shock of it would have been cushioned and rendered less harmful by the fact that they were young; since life for them would swiftly move on, and they would find the diversion of new experiences a rapid antidote for their pain, enabling them to cope with its negativity in a not too self-destructive manner.

For how long the two of them would live, neither of them could tell. Such is the play of chance upon people's lives, that one, or perhaps both of them, could have been dead within a year. However, it would seem more kind and fair to think the opposite, and to wish them a long and happy life, and to believe that whatever stories theirs were to be, they would prove, if one had to relate them, to be less unorthodox tales than this one.